TRAI

TRAFFIC JAM

John McLean

Winter Productions Limited

Copyright © John McLean 1991.

Published by Winter Productions Limited.

ISBN 1872970 01X

Cover design: Jonathan Platt.

Printed and bound in Singapore for Winter Productions Limited, Oak Walk, Saint Peter, Jersey, Channel Islands, by C.W. Printing, Block 31, Defu L:ane 10, #04-70, Singapore 1953.

About the Author

John McLean, who claims with an unconvincing grin that he wrote the whole book while stuck in a traffic jam between Paddington and Wembley, was called to the Bar at Gray's Inn and is now engaged in international commerce. He has university degrees in both Law and History.

His first novel, <u>Island of the Gods</u>, which is set in Bali, was published in 1990. He is a former Naval Reserve officer whose main leisure time activity is surfing.

For John and Diana

By The Same Author

"Island of the Gods." A classic love story set on the island of Bali. 578 pages. Price: $3-99. Published by Winter Productions Limited, Oak Walk, Saint Peter, Jersey, Channel Islands.

Interwined in the love affair between Adrian, an Australian surfer, and Dayu, a Balinese village girl, are the antics of a Paris lawyer, a Wimbledon finalist, an Italian contessa, a Vietnam veteran, a punk rocker and several other colourful characters.

The richly depicted background is distinctly Balinese — temple dancing, cock-fighting, reincarnation, the ever present spirits and, of course, the wonderful waves which they all ride like gods.

"It's a good read. He's a natural story-teller."
- Kevin Sinclair, Hong Kong Standard.

"Mystery, romance, witchcraft - all bring their share of drama to this tale of the world of surfers."
- Cornish Guardian.

"Any surfer worth his salt will find this book hard to put down.........full of incredible imagery........you can almost hear the waves breaking at Uluwatu.........The author's style of writing makes for light, captivating reading.........Once you begin reading Island of the Gods you will not rest until you have finished the final lines."

- Simon Wootton, Wavelength Magazine.

Chapter One

When Myles Padstow woke up on the morning of Saturday, 17th February, 1990, he was not in the best of moods. The first thing he saw when he opened his eyes was the thick bundle of papers that constituted the brief that his clerk had given him the previous afternoon. He recalled the gleeful look in the young brat's eyes as he handed the papers over. "Here you are, sir. Your case for Monday. Should keep you busy all week-end. I'll think of you on Saturday afternoon when I'm at White Hart Lane watching Spurs beat the boots off Nottingham Forest."

"That's the trouble with being a barrister," thought Myles. "So many solicitors wait until the last moment to deliver the brief and then expect you to drop everything and interrupt your social engagements and stand up in court on Monday with all the facts and legal arguments at one's fingertips. And a wretched conspiracy case; they're always the hardest to master."

At twenty-seven Myles was the third youngest member of his chambers and one of the rising stars at the junior criminal Bar where his skilful advocacy and economy with words kept the attention of juries and often got his client off the hook. Legally, of course. He worked out at a gym two nights a week where he put his six foot one athletic frame through all sorts of excruciatingly painful exercises as he sought to keep his muscles working and his figure trim.

He had inherited the fair hair of his mother's Viking forebears as opposed to the darker features of his paternal ancestors who were descended from a knight in armour who came over with

1

the Conqueror in 1066. The Viking features were not the only gifts that he had inherited from his mother. Her creative instincts had rendered her a poetess of considerable accomplishment and there was a wild and unconventional streak in her character which always made her the life of the party. And this rather reckless sense of *joie de vivre* was also to be found in her fun loving and thrill seeking son. Myles was both charming and bohemian; the former quality was always a distinct advantage in the small world of the Bar; the latter less so.

His father was more conservative and stuffy. The quintessential City type who, like a glorified bookie, made his money out of insurance by assessing what sort of odds should be placed against a risk not eventuating. The only risk that he never insured against was that of his son having a motor bike crash. "Wouldn't have it on my professional conscience to put any of my clients up to insuring against that," he used to say as Myles and his friends from the age of seventeen onwards used to roar up and down the undulating country lane in deepest Sussex in which the Padstow house was situated.

"Can't see the point of paying for him to go to public school if all he wants to do is come home and ride that death machine with all the village hoons. Whatever will he do with his life? Become a motor cycle courier delivering letters in the City?" But Myles was smarter than that.

He went up to Oxford, did a law degree and then passed with distinction his Bar Final exams at Gray's Inn. And now he was earning more than his father. But he still rode motor-bikes. Just for fun. But not this week-end. And all because of the wretched last minute brief that his clerk had given him.

However, the case of the difficult brief was not the only knife that had cut into what had promised to be a thoroughly enjoyable week-end. There had also been the little matter of the rugby ticket which had occurred on Thursday night.

Some distant Padstow uncle had arrived from Australia and Myles had done the decent thing and taken the old boy out to dinner at his club. It was Uncle Douglas' first trip back to England since 1940 when he arrived as an eager nineteen year old, fresh from his flying course at the Empire Air Training School in Rhodesia and ready to do battle with Hitler's Luftwaffe for the supremacy of the skies over southern England. His score was eight certain hits and two "not confirmed" — oh, and a Distinguished Flying Cross. The next year he was posted to Malta and then to Burma and at the end of the War he settled down on a sheep farm in the Hunter Valley of New South Wales and was not heard of again. Until now. Recently widowed, he had sold his sheep station, embarked upon a world trip and turned up in England which, he kept saying, was "much changed from when I was last here".

Myles had enjoyed his dry humour and natural charm. And his innocent naïvety — especially when he complained about having to stand in the queue at Heathrow for "Others".

"I can tell you, Myles, it didn't impress me to see all the Indians and the blacks — and even the Germans — being waved through while I was put with the aliens. I don't want it to look as if I'm moaning but it did leave a bit of a sour taste. After all, Australians are British too—same flesh and blood and same Queen. I wasn't treated like that when I arrived in 1940."

"No, you wouldn't have been. The present restrictions are a result of the Commonwealth Immigration Act which was inteneded to keep out all the blacks and Indians but the spineless types who introduced it went and included our own kith and kin in the white dominions — the ones who fought for us in the War. Like yourself."

"And to make matters worse," said Douglas, "I want to go to Twickenham on Saturday and I can't get a ticket for love or money. I've always been a keen rugby follower and there's nothing I'd like more than to see the Springboks play the British Lions at Twickenham. To tell you the truth I never went along with all that sports boycott nonsense and neither did any of my friends. It was mostly the politicians and the church people and I've never

3

had much time for those types. Too interfering for my liking. But now that South Africa is back in world rugby I want to see them play. And what an occasion! To see the British Lions play in Britain for the first time. That's what I've never understood about British rugby. You've sent some great Lions teams abroad but the British people never get to see them play at home. At least not as a team. Just England, Ireland, Scotland and Wales. That's what makes Saturday's match such a special one."

It was all too much for Myles. He pulled his wallet out of his pocket, extracted the precious ticket for which he had paid a king's ransom and handed it to Uncle Douglas.

The old boy's face lit up like a Christmas tree. "Are you sure you don't mind? I mean, I'm not depriving you of anything, am I?"

"No, it's my pleasure. We are always pleased to see our colonial cousins. I'll probably be able to get another one." But he knew that he couldn't.

■
———

As he leapt out of the four-poster bed to take a shower Myles looked down at Fiona, his other half, who was just beginning to stir. They had been together for the last six months which, he reflected, had been so mutually satisfying that it wouldn't be long before he popped the question.

With her long flaxen hair, lively eyes and flawless complexion Fiona was one of London's most successful photograhic models who posed for only the most prestigious cameramen and best paid advertisements. She was still young and naïve enough to be a romantic and appeared to be genuinely thrilled by everything she saw. She took a great interest in Myles' criminal cases and never tired of hearing about the plot, the charge, the conspiracy, the forensic evidence, the lying witnesses, the sobbing victim, the bloodthirsty murderer, the stern old judge and the twelve bored faces on the jury who seemed to be wondering what it was all about.

4

Fiona came from Leicestershire. Her father, a yeoman farmer, fattened bullocks on his broad acres. He was master of the local Hunt and all his daughters (there were six of them)had spent most of their early life in the saddle — at pony club meetings, gymkhanas or just riding along the beautiful hedged lanes of the countryside. On her seventeenth birthday Fiona cancelled her subscription to Horse and Hound and took one out for Vogue instead. Young men came to replace horses in her affections with the result that she now rode only occasionally with her father's fashionable Shire pack.

She arrived in London at the age of eighteen to do a secretarial course in Knightsbridge. However, it took her only a short time to decide that a life of sitting in an office playing with typewriters, telephones and the boss was not for her.

Her first break into modelling came at a dinner party in Hampstead one night when she sat next to an advertising agent who told her that she had just the look that he was seeking for a series of sportswear commercials. She was engaged on the spot. The sportswear company was more than happy with the result and sent her to Los Angeles for a further series of shootings. It wasn't long before the contracts were coming in thick and fast and Fiona applied herself to her work with a dedication that was not always to be found in some of the more shallow and flighty girls who were in it only for the glamour.

Her first serious boyfriend had been a hairdresser in the King's Road who was gentle, polite and dull. Then she had a relationship with a racing car driver who, whenever he had too much to drink, abused her terribly. Which was why, when she met Myles at a mutual friend's party at Wimbledon, she was immediately bowled over by his charm, good looks and slightly bohemian ways. Unlike some other barristers, whose only excitement in life is to bore dinner parties with tales of the vicarious exploits of their criminal clients, Myles was into living life to the full himself. There was a certain weird and fatal attraction about him which Fiona found irresistible.

She too was full of fun and Myles found her refreshing, obliging and unpredictable — and always a delight to be with. Especially last night when she draped his black barrister's gown over her see-through nightie, put on his wig, chased him all round the house and then made love on the couch — still wearing the wig. "This is how they must have done it in the time of Queen Anne," she kept laughing.

"Well, Queen Anne must have done it all the time; she had loads of children — even though most of them died at birth," replied her lover.

But that was last night. There seemed little cause for cheer on this unlucky Saturday morning. Even the weather looked miserable as he stood at the window and looked across the square. The first leaves of spring were beginning to appear on the elms and plane trees and he wondered how much longer the cold would last. He put on his jeans, two pullovers and a trench coat and walked across the square to the Welsh dairy on the corner to buy a copy of the Daily Windbag.

"Are you going to the rugby, Mister Padstow?" asked old Ivor who was the third generation of his family to run the shop.

"No, unfortunately. I gave my ticket away."

"My God! You must be the most generous man in London."

"More likely the biggest fool."

Back at the house he made a cup of tea, took one into Fiona — who had fallen asleep again — and then sat down at the kitchen table to read the paper. He started at the back and read an illuminating preview of the big match at Twickenham before turning to the soccer page. For the first time in living memory all the main London teams were playing home matches. Crystal Palace was playing Manchester United at Selhurst Park, Chelsea was pitted against Liverpool at Stamford Bridge, West Ham were at home to Sunderland, Wimbledon against Aston Villa at Wimbledon, Arsenal were playing Coventry at Highbury, Queen's Park Rangers were at home to Sheffied United, Watford against Bristol City at Vicarage Road Stadium, Millwall were playing

6

Plymouth at Cold Blow Lane, Fulham were at Craven Cottage against Everton, Brentford were at home to Exeter City and, as Myles' clerk had so tactlessly reminded him, Spurs were hosts to Forest.

He turned to the Entertainment Page which was dominated by a big photo of Jerry Garcia of the Grateful Dead strumming away on an electric guitar. "Damn! If I'd known that the Dead were playing to-night at Wembley Arena I would have bought a ticket. Too late now," he thought as he read that the concert had been sold out for more than a week. Below that was a preview of the massive show at Wembley Stadium where the Bumble Bees of Birmingham were playing to seventy-eight and a half thousand fans.

The Bumble Bees had been billed as Birmingham's answer to Liverpool's Beatles although Myles couldn't understand why — since all they seemed to do was to "Buzzzzz" all the time as they pranced around the stage with wings on. Then the audience took up the cry and started to "Buzzzzz" back until there was a dreadful buzzing drone that could be heard for miles around and was reputed to confuse the birds to such an extent that several of them had committed suicide by drowning in the ornamental ponds at Trafalgar Square.

Myles then turned to the front page of the paper where the lead story was that all the train drivers on Britain Rail and London Underground would be on strike from 6 a.m. "However," the report continued, "British Rail drivers will not stop their trains in the middle of the tracks. So as not to inconvenience their passengers they will drive them to the mainline London stations and then go on strike." The article stated that the reason for the strike was to ensure the safety of the guards, drivers and inspectors. "This follows the stabbing of an inspector on the Piccadilly Line last night. Mister George Wheels (better known as 'Bruiser the Cruiser' — the heavyweight boxer) was stabbed several times in the face by a football hooligan and is in a serious condition in St. Mary's Hospital. The train drivers and guards have said that they

7

have had enough of football supporters and that the stabbing of Mr. Wheels was the last straw. In view of the large football crowds expected to turn out in London this afternoon the railway unions say that they fear further attacks on their members and so have gone on strike to prevent even more dastardly deeds. We say that this is one strike that is completely justified and the sooner that capital punishment is brought in for football hooligans the better."

What the report failed to mention was the background to the incident. The problem was that most of the drivers and guards wanted to go to the football but the tight rosters prevented them from doing so. Accordingly they decided to take the matter into their own hands by provoking an incident and thereby giving them an apparently justifiable excuse to go on strike. And Bruiser, by virtue of his fighting record, had been chosen as the fall guy to do the dirty work. It was felt that he was the best one to take a knock.

He picked on a thin young man who was on his own in a carriage listening to a Walkman. The passenger had extremely short hair, oil stained jeans, a large leather jacket and several earrings studded through both ears. "He'll do," thought Bruiser as he stamped menacingly down the carriage. "What are you looking at me like that for?" he scowled at the passenger.

The man turned off his Walkman, looked up in surprise and said, "I beg your pardon. I didn't hear what you said."

"You deaf or something?" Whack! Bruiser brought his heavy, fat fist fist down and smashed him in the cheek. Just below the left eye.

The man was both surprised and hurt. His street-wise mind told him to strike back in self-defence but then, quick as lightning, he realised that he would come off second best in any scuffle with such a giant. So he pulled out the long bladed knife that was concealed in the inside pocket of his jacket and stabbed Bruiser in the face. Then again. And then in the neck. Blood spurted out and stained the cushion of the newly upholstered seat. The big man fell to the floor with a thump just as the train pulled into a station. The passenger pulled the knife out of Bruiser's bloody neck and put it

8

back inside the jacket. Then he darted out the doors, along the platform and up the escalator before anyone could chase him.

Fortunately for Bruiser an off-duty nurse got on at the other end of the carriage, saw the big mass of humanity lying on the floor and rushed to the scene. She called out to the platform attendant, "Quick. Ring 999."

There wasn't a telephone in the station that was operative and so the little man had to run up the escalator, rush through the ticket barrier and along the footpath to the crowded bar of the Goose and Gander public house where, above the din of the merry patrons, he eventually got through to the operator and an ambulance arrived soon afterwards. Such was the incident which sparked the Great Rail Strike.

Even without the rail strike the number of cars converging on London for the football was expected to be a record. And therein lay some more mischief. In the recent local body elections the councils of Central London had been taken over by extreme left wing zealots who, if they had their way, would deprive every Englishman of his right to drive a motor car. They maintained that all the evils of modern city living were caused by the internal combustion engine and that people should give up their cars and use public transport instead. That argument might have been a bit more persuasive if public transport was up to scratch but, as everyone knew, it wasn't. And so, to these anti-motorist councils, the expected heavy traffic of Saturday, 17th February, was a godsend.

They decided to exploit it in order to turn up the heat in their war against car owners. And what Myles read next in the paper made him really angry. "In their latest strike against the right to drive a car the new left wing councils have decided to take advantage of the expected heavy traffic to impose what they call 'controlled congestion' on all bridges across the Thames as well as the Dartford and Blackwall tunnels. This means that every bridge will be reduced to a single lane. Lights will regulate the flow but, as traffic comes across one way, there will be a bank-up of cars going in the opposite direction. Their stated aim is to 'drive the motorists out of their cars and on to public transport.' In the absence of the Secretary of State of Transport, who has already left for his country house in Devon, the Under-Secretary has roundly criticised the move as 'the latest example of the Loony Left's irresponsibility' but such words are not expected to be of much comfort to the motorists affected."

Myles turned the page and glanced at the photograph beneath the main headline. It was a picture of the President of France with a grave expression on his face. The accompanying article stated that he was flying to Chequers by helicopter during the afternoon to have urgent consultations with Mrs. Thatcher about the latest crisis in the Gulf. Yet another Moslem madman had emerged in the southern part of the Arabian Peninsula and the British and the Americans were desperately trying to bring the French in on the Allied side so as to have the use of the French base at nearby Djibouti. The President had at last agreed to fly to England with his wife and Mrs. Thatcher was counting on persuading him to allow the Allies into Djibouti.

Beneath this article was a small paragraph about the United States Lawyers' Conference which was being held in London and which was being attended by a record number of fifteen thousand American attorneys and judges.

The telephone rang. "That you, Myles?"

"Yes."

"It's Jackal here. Some of us in the chapter have decided to go for a run down the A40 this afternoon. Care to join us?"

"Unfortunately I've got a lot of work to do. I'm defending a chap in a conspiracy trial on Monday and I haven't even looked at the brief."

"What's the substantive charge?"

"Receiving stolen goods."

"Gee, I'll help you with that. Me mate was once charged with that one and he got off. Kept the goods too. If you tell us the guts of it, we'll tell you how to get him off."

"Well, I'd sure like to come. I haven't been on a decent ride since my engine was reconditioned. If you remember rightly I missed the last rally because of 'flu. But what about the traffic? It's going to be hellish with all these football supporters and now the trains are on strike."

Jackal laughed. "Has traffic ever deterred the Hell's Angels? We'll just weave our way in and out of all the drivers and scare the living daylights out of them. Make eyes at all their spunky daughters — like we always do."

"You've tempted me. What time are we meeting? And where?"

"Twelve o'clock. That's midday — not midnight. We'll gather in the usual place. Parliament Square. Just in front of Churchill's statue."

"Yes," thought Myles as he put down the receiver. "That's just what I need to cheer me up. A nice run down the A40 and back with the boys. I'll start on the brief to-night."

His membership of the Western Districts Chapter of Hell's Angels went back several years to when he had defended a bunch of them on a charge of affray. His eloquence in court had got them all off and they were so delighted that they asked him to be an honorary member of their chapter and to go for a ride with them on the following Sunday. Which he did.

Myles had always enjoyed the thrill of riding a motor-bike and had invested some of his earnings in a powerful Harley Davidson Sportster which he kept at the back of his garage. He enjoyed that first ride and insisted on joining up as a fully paid member. The others were delighted to have a barrister in their gang in spite of the condition that he imposed on his membership. Namely, that if ever any of them got into trouble with the law, he would not be prepared to defend them in court.

"Why is that, Guv? Don't want to be publicly associated with us?"

"No, it's not that at all," he replied in all honesty. "It's just that — well, if we ride together, we'll become friends. And it's not good for a barrister to defend anyone whom he knows well. Not good for the client. You see, the best thing that a barrister has to offer is his fresh and independent advice. And, if I know you well, that would affect my judgement. I wouldn't be able to do justice to your case."

In the event the matter was largely academic as the Angels had long since become respectable and more or less law-abiding except that some of them still insisted on throwing off their crash helmets as soon as they reached the edge of London and began to inhale the sweet and sometimes earthy scents of the countryside. They didn't see what right the authorities had to force them to have their heads imprisoned in a helmet; they preferred to ride as free as the air they breathed and with their hair flying in the wind. And the cops couldn't do a thing about it; their bikes were quite gutless compared to what the Angels rode.

Fiona was now wide awake and was standing naked in front of the bathroom mirror. "Myles, be a sweetie and turn up the central heating. Otherwise I'll have to go and put some clothes on," she called.

"That would be terrible. I'd have to throw you out," he replied as he walked across the room to turn the knob.

"And do let's have some music. The place is as silent as a morgue." He turned on the stereo. "Not so loud, Mylo. I've only just got up. I had this amazing dream. You know that car of your's — the French one."

"It's actually a Renault GTA Sports."

"Yes, well I'm not very knowledgeable on cars. All I know is that it's French. I dreamt that I was driving it along the King's Road and there was so much traffic that I was travelling about five miles an hour. And all the shopkeepers came running out of their shops with hundred franc notes in their hands and they started giving them to me — pushing them through the windows and sticking them on the outside of the car with Scotch tape. There must have been thousands of them. You see, the French car attracted French money. Has that ever happened to you when you've been driving in the King's Road?"

"No, not yet."

"Oh, do change the tape. You know I can't stand Madonna."

"What about Dire Straits? Perhaps 'Money for Nothing, Chicks for Free'? It might help us to realise the dream."

"Oh, what a good idea!"

"I'm going for a run with the Angels at twelve o'clock. What's your programme for the day?"

"I'm meeting Annabelle and we're going shopping in the Portobello Road."

"What? Another antique chamber pot for the flowers?"

"No. Annabelle's looking for a chastity belt. Says she's terrified of becoming pregnant."

"I'm not surprised; she's such a nymphomaniac."

"Don't be so beastly. Who says that?"

"The whole male gender."

"Maybe we can take your car since you won't be using it?"

"Of course. Just don't go across the river. The councils are blocking all the bridges."

"Why?"

"To try to upset the motorists so much that we'll stop using our cars."

"Sounds pretty stupid to me."

"Yes, but unfortunately you get some very stupid people on the councils."

"How cold is it outside?"

"Freezing."

"Then I'll have to put two pairs of leg warmers on."

"Like hell you will. Those things should be banned for any woman under eighty."

When she emerged from the *en suite* she was wearing only the leg warmers and nothing else. Myles tugged at the dreadful looking things and peeled them down her wildly kicking legs. "You look much better without them," he laughed as he gave her a playful slap on the buttocks.

13

He grabbed the ghastly pieces of wool and took them downstairs to the garage. "They'll make nice, soft rags for polishing the bike," he called back to Fiona who was now struggling to pull a pair of silver tights up her well-shaped legs.

"They look much better," he grinned as he came back from the garage and threw the oil stained leggings into the rubbish container. "You should wear silver all the time. It suits you. Can you make some coffee while I go and get my leathers on. It's already twenty past eleven and we're meeting at twelve at Westminster."

Myles pulled on the tight black leather pants and tied them up the sides to make them even tighter. Then he picked up his studded leather jacket with the Hell's Angels logo hand painted on the back. There was a row of silver studs down the outside of the sleeves and a small skull and crossbones painted in white on the front right hand side. The jacket had been a gift from an earlier Angel who had borrowed a hundred pounds from him during a rally and then couldn't repay.

After Myles had finished his coffee he put on the jacket, zipped it up tight and went to kiss Fiona good-bye. "You look really great in leather," she drooled. "Suits you much better than your wig and gown."

"It feels better too."

"May I ride pillion with you on one of your rallies?"

"No way. Not when I'm riding with the chapter."

"Why not?"

"They might be my riding friends but I wouldn't be so stupid as to let someone as good-looking as you anywhere near them. They're not all....well...um.... gentlemen."

"But they're your friends?"

"Oh, yes. We all get along famously. They're wild, loose, free-thinking, fun-loving guys. I always enjoy being with them. They laugh at everything and have no respect for convention or authority. I find it quite refreshing. I'd far rather spend an afternoon with the Angels than with some of my colleagues in chambers. Not all of them, mind you. Some of the other barristers are really great chaps. But I have to be serious all the week so I like to kick loose at week-ends."

"Sounds like fun to me. You should bring them all back here one evening and we could have a party."

"No way."

He gave a her a peck on the cheek, picked up his crash helmet and made his way to the garage. Then, with a roar of acceleration that he knew always annoyed the other residents of the well-heeled square, he was on his way. But not for long.

He had to stop at the first set of lights that was showing red. As he drew to a halt he looked up and down the roads of the intersection which were crowded with cars as far as the eye could see. Even when the lights turned green nothing moved. Indeed, nothing could move — except the pedestrians, the bicycles and the motor-bikes.

Myles could see a narrow lane between the cars so he broke through the light — which had turned red again — and weaved his way in and out of the traffic. The main road was completely blocked by all manner of cars, trucks and vans so he turned into a side street on the left and rode towards Victoria. Drivers were becoming impatient and the cacophony of car horns could be heard for miles.

Everything was at a standstill around Victoria as the bank-up of cars from the council blocked Vauxhall Bridge stretched right to the station and beyond. All the lanes of Victoria Street were jam packed with vehicles that had been sitting bumper to bumper for more than an hour. He sped along the footpath and narrowly missed colliding with an obese policewoman who was waddling out of Scotland Yard.

When he reached Parliament Square he wended his way through the motionless traffic to the Churchill statue where the other members of the chapter were gathered.

"Hi lads," he called as he brought his machine to a gentle halt at the foot of the statue that was still covered with wilting wreaths that had been placed there three weeks earlier on the anniversary of the great man's death.

"Hell, have you seen all the traffic? It's wild, man! Never seen anything like it," said Jackal. "Anyway now that we're all here we may as well get on our way. It'll be slow going to get to the A40 but then we can go hell for leather. Let's turn off at High Wycombe and go to that little country pub in Buckinghamshire where they have the topless waitresses. You know, the one we drank dry last Bank Holiday week-end." They formed up in a single line and started on their way. Myles was at Number Seven. He looked up at Big Ben. It was ten minutes past twelve.

Chapter Two

As might be expected, the office of the Chief Commander of London Traffic was not the happiest place to be on 17th February, 1990. The newly appointed Commander, Cyril Thicknesse, was an ex-bouncer who had joined the force under its Mature Entrants' Scheme. He had been promoted to the position of Commander a week earlier after his predecessor had been run over and killed on his way home from a Road Safety Conference.

The new Commander had had his inauguration booze-up in the cops' cafeteria the night before and was nursing an extremely sore head, to say nothing of an upset stomach. By eleven o'clock, when the first reports of the traffic began to filter through to his desk, he realised that he was in for a baptism of fire.

He made a few 'phone calls and then ordered a large number of his officers to direct the traffic outside the soccer ground where his own team was playing. That would enable most of the club's supporters to get to the game and cheer the team on and he would reveal his heroic role at the next club meeting. They might even make him a Life Member.

At ten past twelve the telephone rang. "Commander Thicknesse here. Whadda ya want?"

"Good morning, Commander. Or should I say, Good afternoon. Telford-Weston here. Editor of the Daily Troublemaker."

"Just what I need!" thought Thicknesse as he downed another aspirin in a vain attempt to get rid of his hangover.

"I'm just ringing to ask you if you have any comment to make on our lead story for to-morrow's Sunday edition."

"What's the story?"

"The story is, Commander, that this whole dreadful traffic jam, that now affects the whole of London, was caused by a broken down Mercedes on the Wembley turn-off of the A40."

"I have not had any report on that."

"No, I don't suppose you would have—considering that your officers seem to be entirely to blame for the whole affair."

"Whadda ya mean?"

"A dark blue Mercedes broke down on the Wembley round-about between Hanger Lane and the North Circular Road shortly after ten o'clock this morning. It was travelling in the centre lane. The driver, a City gent who is prepared to back up the story, got out and lifted his bonnet to try to ascertain what the problem was. The traffic was starting to bank up behind him but the other lanes were still flowing freely. Then a police car came by and pulled up beside the Mercedes to see what was wrong, thereby blocking another lane of traffic.

The driver of the Mercedes, acting like a responsible citizen, asked the police to call up the R. A. C. on their radio. But oh no, they were too clever for that. Amateur mechanics, you see. The one chance in their lives to look under the bonnet of a Mercedes and tamper with the parts. For half an hour they had their heads under the bonnet and all the time the traffic was banking up and blocking two lanes instead of one.

Then a couple of motor-bike cops weaved their way through the slow moving lanes and parked their bikes in the middle of the only lane that was still moving. One of them got into the Mercedes and started playing with all the pedals and gadgets while the other one just sat there and ran his hand over the smooth suede seats. Don't forget, their two colleagues still had their big heads under the bonnet."

"How do you know all this?"

"Our Chief Reporter's wife was in the car behind the Mercedes. Taking her children to the pictures."

"Oh Christ!" groaned the Commander as he wiped his sweating brow.

"Cars were starting to toot and some of the drivers began abusing the cops and told them to get a move on.

This only made them dig their toes in and they said that they would remove their vehicles when it suited them and not before. One of them then asked to see everybody's driver's licence to see if they were up-to-date. By now the cars were banked up all along the A40 as far as Uxbridge in the west and Paddington in the east where they merged with all the traffic that was lined up to get across the blocked bridges. The North Circular Road is now blocked all round and not a single vehicle is moving north of the river. And not much south of it either. Do you have any comment to make on these matters?"

"No comment," said the Commander, "other than to say that we in this office do not accept that there is a traffic jam. It is merely heavy traffic congestion."

"Then would you accept that the whole of London is in a state of gridlock?"

"No, that's an American word; we don't use it over here. And it is not true to say that the traffic is not moving. It is. I've just had a report that vehicles on the Embankment have advanced three and a half feet in the last two hours."

"Just like on the Western Front eh? Where it took four years to advance a couple of miles. Backwards and forwards the line went."

"It's not at all like the Western Front. So far the traffic hasn't moved backwards. What movement that has taken place has been in a forward direction. I have not had any reports of widespread reversing."

"Thank you, Commander. I shall mention your total lack of co-operation in to-morrow's story. By the way, how do you spell 'Thickness'? Is it with an 'e' on the end or without?"

"With an 'e'. My grandfather added the 'e' by deed poll." He slammed the receiver down and ran out to the toilet to throw up. His hangover was getting worse.

When he returned he tapped Mr. Telford-Weston's name

into the computer to find out his address and car number plate. He wrote the details down and diarised the matter for Monday when he would place a discreet twenty-four hour police watch on Telford-Weston's movements so as to nab him on a drink driving charge.

■
_____

Although the Commander and his team of advisers were unable to agree on how to unlock the "heavy traffic congestion" there was no disagreement about the priority for dealing with the matter: the first task was to find someone to blame for causing the problem in the first place; the second was to unjam the traffic.

"Who can we blame?" screamed the Commander. "Has to be some species that won't have the public and press rushing to its aid."

"But isn't it the fault of the left wing councillors who blocked all the bridges?" asked Assistant Commander Dullard.

"We mustn't blame them. Doesn't pay to get off-side with those types. You never know when they might pop up as Home Secretary or Chancellor in a future Labour Government and we'd be dependent on them for our funds. And our pensions."

"You mean it's possible that that nodding ginger-nut from Wales with the funny accent might one day become Prime Minister?"

"Yes, if the people are stupid enough to vote for him and want to have their taxes increased. And we can't blame the present government for not building more roads because at the moment we're dependent on them for our funds."

"What about blaming the football crowds? I mean, they're all pouring into London in their hundreds of thousands and making things worse."

"No," replied the Commander, "it is not the fault of the football supporters." He knew that his club would never make him a Life Member if he came out against football fans..

The telephone rang again. It was his Chief of Operations.

"Excuse me, Commander, but I have a couple of problems to discuss with you. There are now more cars around Saint John's Wood and Lords than I've ever seen for a cricket Test. I've just had a call from Lords and apparently there's a meeting about to start in the Committee Room and some of the people are unable to get there because of the traffic."

"Oh Christ!" said the Commander. "There go all our free Test tickets for next summer. When they see that we can't handle the traffic on an ordinary Saturday they're hardly likely to feel the need to butter us up to control the cars on a Test day."

"I wouldn't let that worry you."

"Well it does. I love cricket but I'm damned if I'm going to pay to get in."

"But the people going to the meeting won't be able to see the traffic."

"Whadda you mean?"

"Although they're using the Committee Room, it's not a meeting of the M. C. C. Committee."

"What is it then?"

"The Annual General Meeting of the Blind Cricket Umpires' Association."

"How many of them?"

"About a hundred."

"Is that all? I would have thought there'd be thousands."

"I don't think that every blind umpire actually joins the association."

"Right, well that explains it. Now what's your second problem?"

"What am I going to do about all the people who will be coming to Wembley to-night for the concerts? The Bumble Bees are playing at Wembley Stadium. Full house — seventy-eight and a half thousand — and the Grateful Dead are at Wembley Arena and they've been sold out for more than a week."

The Commander knew all about the Bumble Bees. "But who the hell are the Grateful Dead?" he asked. "In fact, I'd be grateful to be dead myself at the moment."

"The Grateful Dead, sir, are one of the oldest rock bands in the States. Been going since the mid Sixties and they still draw the crowds. Seems they have their own solid core of fans, who are called 'Deadheads', and these Deadheads follow the band around everywhere it plays. All over America and now they've come to Europe for this winter tour. There were eleven thousand tickets for the concert and apparently ten thousand of them have been bought by these American Deadheads. Our own people can hardly get a look in."

"Well they will to-night. Most of the Americans won't be able to get through the traffic and so there should be plenty of spare seats."

"I wouldn't be too sure of that."

"Why?"

"Because large numbers of these Deadheads are already at Wembley and are waiting outside the Arena in their vans. Some of them have been sleeping there for two nights. It's quite a carnival atmosphere — you know, guys selling hand-made leather belts and their girl-friends knitting woollen bikinis and all that. There's a great long line of vans that are parked all the way down to the North Circular Road."

"How many?"

"I'd say about three hundred."

"Could we say a thousand?"

"I don't see why not."

"Splendid! And it was this concentration of vans that caused the heavy congestion which now encompasses the whole of London?"

"Oh, I wouldn't go that far."

"Do you want to keep your job as Chief of Operations or would you like me to put you back on the beat? I'll repeat the question. It was this concentration of vans that has caused the traffic congestion all over London, was it not?"

"Yes sir, it was."

The Commander put down the receiver. He turned to his bunch of advisers, the smallest of whom was fifteen and a half stone, and said, "We're saved, chaps. At least we've found somebody to blame for the congestion. And that 'somebody' is a genus that can not possibly rebound on us. A bunch of young hippies from America who have come over here to attend a concert by some group called the Grateful Dead. With a name like that you can imagine what they must be like. No none will take their side. They're not voters and they don't even live here. And they're all sitting in their vans up at Wembley *blocking the traffic*."

"But how can you be sure that they've caused all the congestion?" asked the sceptical Assistant Commander.

"It's not a matter of proving it, Dullard. We're not going to charge them in court. All we have to do is throw enough mud for some of it to stick."

"But what if the American ambassador complains? I mean, it does sound rather discriminatory."

"He won't complain. Not at the moment. Don't forget, they're trying to butter us up to let our armoured brigades in the desert serve under the command of their General McMurgatroyd."

"Which General McMurgatroyd is that? General Harry McMurgatroyd or General Mary McMurgatroyd?"

"The latter. The one whom the President called 'the General Patton of the Nineties'. Now, are we all agreed that it is safe to blame these Dead people for causing all the congestion?"

"Agreed!" They all shook hands and patted each other on their broad backs.

"And now to the second matter. How do we get rid of this congestion?" asked Assistant Commander Dullard.

"Not yet!" cried the Commander. "I feel as sick as a dog. Give me an hour. I'll go for a walk. It's lunchtime anyway and we never work in the lunch hour." They broke up and agreed to reconvene at quarter past two.

The Commander decided to take a stroll to the betting shop to put ten pounds for a win on *Craphappy Jappy* which was running in the hurdles at Worcester. "Besides," he thought, "it'll give me a chance to have a look at the traffic — first hand."

Inside the betting shop he looked up at the blackboard and was surprised to see a long list of times in one column with ever lengthening odds alongside each hour. What the Supreme Commander of London Traffic was staring at was nothing less than the list of odds that were being offered to punters on when the traffic jam would end.

"It can't go on much longer," he heard one of them say. "The police must have it under control soon. And then everything will start flowing normally again."

"Horse punters to Windows One to Five, traffic punters Windows Six to Ten please," called the betting shop manager.

The Commander stood in the queue for the horses, which was definitely the shorter line, and stared in amazement at the scene in front of Windows Six to Ten. People were struggling to hand over wads of notes in return for betting slips with the appropriate odds. "Twenty pounds on 2.30 p.m., ten pounds on five o'clock and fifty on 6.15 to-night!" screamed one woman who was pulling an empty shopping basket on wheels — presumbly to put the money in and wheel it home.

Commander Thicknesse might have been slow at some things but when it came to the Main Chance he was just as fast as anyone else. He had joined the police force to make money and to-day looked more propitious than any other.

When he reached the front of the queue and handed over ten pounds the friendly lady behind the window looked up and smiled. "I thought you'd be over at the other window, Commander. After all, you are in charge of traffic, aren't you?"

"Yes, madam, and that is the very reason why I can't go over there. It wouldn't be ethical if you get what I mean."

"Yes, of course. Inside knowledge."

"That's right. We have very high standards in the Force." He checked the betting slip, put it in his wallet and then walked across the road to the red telephone box. He rang his old pal and fellow ex-bouncer, Slick Nick, with whom he had been in and out of several enterprises — some of them lasting only a few minutes — and whom he regarded as a trusted friend. The two men had recently taken their wives to the Caribbean on holiday and often went halves on bets.

"That you, Nick? Me here. Listen mate, I think we've at last struck it. We'll be able to buy that country club we saw in Barbados within a couple of months. You know, the one that's run by that ex-gangster from the East End who gave us the free lunch and said that he'd sell it to us for a couple of million. Along with the beautiful cane furniture and all the black servants who were bowing and scraping to us all through the meal. And an assured clientele during the winter months."

"Yes, but as I said at the time, how the hell could the likes o' you and me afford something as grand as that?"

"I'll tell you. The betting shops are laying odds on how long this wretched traffic congestion will last. And I've just seen their list of odds and they get longer until to-morrow midday when they're offering five hundred to one. Seems everyone thinks that it'll be cleared by nightfall. Of course, I can't go in and place a bet myself because I'd be recognised but, if you play your part and front up at the window with the money — better make it several trips to different windows; don't want to shorten the odds — then I'll do my bit and spin the congestion out until Monday if necessary. If it's already five hundred to one for midday to-morrow then why don't you ask for eleven o'clock Monday morning?"

"You could do that?"

"No sweat."

"But you'll probably lose your job. They'll say that you were incompetent."

"Do you think I care? I only joined this mob to make some money. No way am I going to retire to a semi-detached in Ealing like so many cops are forced to do. This way we can make at least a million each and retire to the Caribbean. No one would ever suspect it."

"But if we're gonna make that sort of money I'm going to have to front up with loads of cash and I've got less than a hundred quid on me until the banks open on Monday."

"Come round and see me at my office as soon as you can and I'll hand you ten thousand pounds."

"You carry that sort of cash on you at week-ends?"

"No, of course not. But I have my contacts."

"Roger. I'll be there by two-thirty."

The Commander strolled back to the building that housed his office but he didn't go up there immediately. Instead, he took the lift down to the basement which had been turned into offices and a bar for a bunch of drug cops who seemed to be a law unto themselves.

"Hello, Cyril, How's the head? That was a damned good booze-up you turned on for us all last night. What can we do for you?" asked one of the thuggish looking operatives.

"I was just wondering if you chaps could do me a favour."

"Of course. Anything for a fellow Mason. The only reason we join the Lodge is to help each other get ahead in the world."

"You always have loads of cash floating around, don't you?"

"Too right. We keep a hundred thousand in used notes in the safe over there. Just in case we have to go out and make an undercover drug purchase."

"Well, can you loan me say ten thousand for the week-end? I'll pay you back on ...... Tuesday. How's that?"

"Fine. We're not expecting any action in the next forty-eight hours, are we, boys? We wouldn't be able to get through the traffic anyway. Are you sure that ten's enough? You can have more if you like."

"Okay, make it twenty."

26

"Right you are. It's all in bundles of fifties. Five thousand to a bundle. Here's four bundles."

"Do I have to sign anything?"

"No way. Because we're undercover we're not subject to the usual rules. We can do what we like so long as we nab someone every now and then. We're the ones who ask the questions. No one ever asks us questions. If they did, they'd soon find some drugs planted on them and a long jail sentence to follow."

"Bloody oath!" muttered the Commander under his breath as he walked out. "I'm in the wrong Department. Think how much money those boys could make on the side — confiscating valuable drugs and putting only a portion of them into the court. No wonder they all drive such flash cars. Perhaps I should ask for a departmental transfer — from road traffic to drug traffic. Ha, ha, ha!"

■
———

When he returned to his office Thicknesse placed a further call to his Chief of Operations. "Listen," he said, "if this heavy congestion continues into the night — as it looks like doing — then the number of motoring and drink driving offences will be down to almost zero and we all know what that means. A reduction in the crime rate! We just have to keep those crime figures sky high every year to scare the Treasury and the public into giving us more and more funds. Any levelling off — or horror of horrors! — an *actual reduction* is likely to result in them slashing our annual budget on the grounds that crime is going down and there are more urgent calls on the funds elsewhere.

As you know, Chief, drink driving and motoring offences are by far the easiest way to boost the crime figures. And far more remunerative than all the tedious and boring work involved in investigating burglaries. How long does it take to nab a motorist for drink driving?"

"A few minutes."

"Exactly. And how long do burglary cases take?"

"They can take several days."

"Exactly. And we make hundreds of thousands of pounds every day for the Treasury with all the drink driving fines whereas at the end of a burglary case all we do is return the damned stuff to the silly householder who allowed himself to get robbed in the first place. That's why I don't care a tinker's cuss about burglaries — they're just not worth it. Motoring fines are everything and the drink driving laws are the jewel in our little crown. Therefore, even though to-day's traffic doesn't appear to be moving, I don't want any slackening in the nabbing of drivers for offences. Got it?"

"But, if nothing is moving, how on earth can we charge people? I mean, they won't be speeding or drifting over the white line or failing to stop at lights."

"I know all that, Chief, but you are to make up for it with a drink driving blitz. You know the law as well as I do — 'Drunk in charge of a vehicle'. Even if they're sitting in it with the key in the ignition they can still be slammed for drink driving — provided they're over the limit. And on a day like this I imagine that there are thousands of them nipping into the nearest pub for a Scotch or two to keep warm and then getting back into their cars. Just get your men to go along the lines of stationary vehicles and breathalyse the lot of them. If there's any reduction in the number of motoring offences to-day, then your job is on the line. Understand?

The silly fools won't think that they can be nabbed if they're not actually driving. The element of surprise will be our most effective weapon. And don't give me any of that crap about public relations."

"But surely it's more important to clear the traffic?"

"There is nothing more important than the revenue we get from drink driving offences."

Chapter Three

Shortly before one o'clock some of the mischievous councillors who had blocked the bridges decided to derive some sadistic pleasure out of the situation by going along to watch the plight of the motorists. Dressed in crimpelene suits and driving Skodas they made their way towards Lambeth Bridge which, according to the Midday News, was completely jammed and nothing had moved for more than three hours.

After parking their Skodas a couple of miles away they strutted along the traffic clogged streets with their cameras, determined to make the most of their big day.

One of them, who had risen up from barrow boy to soap box orator to councillor, decided to exploit the angry mood of the people for political purposes. He climbed up on the parapet of the bridge and started railing against the Conservative Government for not building wider roads. "Are you angry?" he roared to the stranded motorists who by this time had got out of their cars to see what all the commotion was about.

"Yes!" they called back.

"And you have every right to be angry." He pointed down river towards Westminister with such a vigorous arm movement that he nearly toppled off the parapet. "It's all their fault. Bloody Tories. At this moment they're probably all sitting on the Terrace of Parliament guzzling champagne and laughing at all o' yous who are stuck out here in the cold in your cars and can't move."

"Hey, I recognise you!" cried an exasperated cab driver. "I voted for you in the last council election and you're one of the bastards who voted for the closing of the bridges. Well I've got news for you, Mister Crimpelene Councillor. You're going straight off this bridge and down to the river and, if you drown, then I guess you'll travel a bit further down until you come across the little red men with their pitchforks."

He threw himself at the councillor and pushed him off the parapet. By now the mood of the crowd was decidedly ugly and they started punching and kicking the other councillors whose crimpelene suits were starting to lose some of their shine.

"Quick! Across the bridge," called the council leader. They made a dash for it, dodging the missiles of petrol cans, jacks and spare tyres that the fed up motorists were hurling at them from behind. Some of the fleet footed drivers gave chase. The councillors ran along Millbank and darted down the first road to the left. They found themselves in Smith Square. They looked around for an open door. There was only one in the whole square so they ran to it as fast as their fat little legs could carry them.

"Let us in!" they screamed at the big, burly, uniformed commissionaire who was standing in the doorway with his arms folded across his ample chest.

"I'm sorry, sir, but this is the Central Office of the Conservative and Unionist Party of Great Britain and I can not let you in without a signed pass."

"But we're Conservatives!" they lied.

"Oh no you're not. Conservatives don't appear in the street in crimpelene suits."

By now the angry pursuers had blocked off all the exits of Smith Square and were moving in on their prey with fire in their bellies. "Ha! Ha!" laughed the commissionaire. "You're trapped! Just like the Graf Spee. I think this going to be the most entertaining spectacle since I was a leading hand on H.M.S. Achilles in the mouth of the River Plate."

■

The boat on which the councillor landed when he fell off the bridge was being steered up the river by Stinker Ratcliffe who played in the scrum for a very social team at Blackheath. He had arranged to meet his scrum mates at the local Dog and Bone public house at midday for a pre-match pint before going on to Twickenham in the Tube. But when he dragged his heavily hungover body into the Dog and Bone's Sportsmen's Bar he was told by Herman the Hooker that, although they all had tickets for the great match, they had no means of getting there.

"You'll just have to go and get your old man's cabin cruiser out of the boat shed and take us all up the river to Twickers," said Herman. "We'll give you a hand to push it down the skids into old Father Thames."

The boat was heavier than usual as a result of all the packs of Tennants Extra and Bass that had been packed into it for the voyage. They pushed it into the river, climbed on board and Stinker started the engine.

The sleek craft weaved its way crookedly up the river in the direction of Tower Bridge. The men on board looked up and gave a hearty cheer to all the cars that were lining the banks while waiting to get into the single available lane of the great London landmark. They waved again to the cars on London Bridge and then had a race up to Blackfriars with a speedboat that was pulling a rubber clad water-skier who was in fact a ticket scalp who had some important business to conduct outside the gates of Twickenham.

As they passed the Houses of Parliament they noticed that the traffic on the river was becoming as clogged as it was on the roads. Stinker and his scrum mates weren't the only rugby supporters who had decided to travel to Twickenham by boat. But they were the only ones to receive a crimpelene clad councillor from above.

"Quick! Give him a beer. He must have hurt his head when he hit the deck."

They snapped open a cold can of Bass and handed it to the groggy and injured missile that had landed so unexpectedly from the sky.

"Wonder which planet he's from?" asked one of them.

"Probably from the sun judging by the shine in his suit."

"Shame he hasn't got a dog collar on; we could return him to his owner."

They heard some shouting from above and looked up to see what was the matter.

"Drown him!" called the men on the bridge. "Chuck him overboard; otherwise he'll sink your boat like an evil spirit."

"He's the reason why none of us can move. He's one of the criminal councillors!"

"No," called back Stinker, "I'm not prepared to throw him overboard. I've got a better idea."

"What idea?"

"Well, you see, we're on our way up the river to Twickenham. We'll be going past the Solid Waste Transfer Station at Wandsworth. I'll drop him off there." A great cheer went up from the bridge.

■
———

All roads to Twickenham were jammed with expensive, late model cars as sixty thousand rugby supporters made their way to the ground for what was being billed as the "match of the century". But they didn't all make it. And it was no better for those who had travelled by boat.

So many had chosen water transport that there was a solid mass of boats from Twickenham all the way down to Fulham. And, of course, a party atmosphere prevailed. People stepped from one boat to another until they reached the river bank from where they could continue their journey on foot. Those who were too drunk to get across the bridge of boats just stayed on their own craft and drank it dry before moving on to another where the drinks were still flowing. And those who accidentally fell into the Thames were fished out by the River Police and returned to their boat of origin.

33

Many of the fed-up occupants of the Rolls Royces, Jaguars and Range Rovers that were stranded on the Twickenham Road soon became resigned to the fact that the game would have to start without them. Those who were furthest away from the ground got out of their shiny cars, opened the boots and pulled out well-stocked picnic hampers. They poured various alcoholic concoctions into all sorts of drinking mugs and sat back in the warmth of their vehicles to listen to the match on the car radio.

Others, who found themselves almost at the Twickenham car-park — but not quite — resorted to various unorthodox tactics to make use of their tickets. In some cars that were full of friends, ex-team mates and drinking buddies they drew straws to see which of them would stay and sit behind the wheel lest by some miracle the traffic might start moving. Others — less optimistic — reasoned that nothing would happen for at least a couple of hours so they just locked their vehicles where they were standing and made their way towards the turnstiles.

Among those who were treading the footpaths to Twickenham was a tall, thin man in a black woollen overcoat and a wide-brimmed bushman's hat. Uncle Douglas, conditioned by a lifetime of farming habits, had risen at dawn, had bacon and eggs in the dining room of his West End hotel and then stepped outside into the early morning air. He was greatly looking forward to the match and also to seeing Twickenham — the home of rugby — for the first time. And, of course, he had the precious ticket in the inside flap of his wallet.

He decided to take an early bus to the west and spend the morning wandering around Kew Gardens before walking the short distance to the match. He let a couple of buses pass and then climbed on to a double-decker which was his preferred mode of travelling around London. "Best sightseeing in the whole town for no more than a bus fare," he had told Myles at dinner.

After strolling around the great glass Palm House at Kew and being duly impressed by both its grandeur and flora, he set off on foot for Twickenham. Along the way he passed the Scrum-

34

magers' Arms, a homely looking thatched roof inn that stood on the edge of Richmond Green. He stepped inside its crowded bar and ordered a ploughman's lunch with a pint of Holt's Mild. There was a warm log fire crackling in the corner and he eventually found a table in an alcove beneath some low black beams. In the convivial and smoky atmosphere he spent the next half hour chatting to a group of high spirited rugby players from Wales who were also on their way to the match.

Then he continued on his way and was utterly amazed at the traffic. There were thousands of cars but nothing was moving. A few of the drivers were tooting madly but the majority were just sitting patiently in their cars and enduring the cold and the boredom with stoicism and a stiff upper lip.

Uncle Douglas watched an old Indian who was plying his wares from car window to car window. Harim, the proprietor of the nearby Hurry Curry House, had tied a tray around his neck with twine and was peddling packs of hot curry to the stranded and — by now — very hungry drivers.

Myles' uncle saw him tap on the windscreen of a shining white Jaguar XJ6 that was being driven by a tall, distinguished looking man with a mop of thick white hair.

Colonel Byng-Moresby had set out from his converted tithe barn in Hampshire at 9 a.m. He had travelled up the M3 on his own at about thirty miles an hour and was just beginning to feel a little peckish. He hadn't bothered to pack a hamper as it was always his habit to arrive at the ground a good two hours before the match and have a bite to eat in the bar between pints with his former brother officers from the Bengal Lancers. But to-day his plans had gone askew due to the wretched traffic.

"Jolly thoughtful of you, old chap," bellowed Colonel Byng-Moresby as he wound down the window. "I could do with a curry. Just like the old days in India!"

"Yes," replied Harim. "My father used to walk up and down the Grand Trunk Road in India selling hot curries to all the fine gentlemen and their memsahibs who rode past in their carriages.

That is how we made enough money to cross the sea and come to England. And I can see that all the men going to Twickenham today are pukka sahibs of the highest type. So different to the soccer hooligans."

"Yes, you're right. Twickers always attracts the cream. There are still two Englands, you know — just as Disraeli said. But it's no longer rich and poor."

"What is it then?"

"Rugby and soccer! That's why people like me come here and the other classes all go and stab themselves at the football grounds. We're the officers; they're the men. Just a shame there's all this damned traffic. Some of us won't be able to get to the ground."

"Ah yes, but it is so good for my business. I have sold more curries in the last half hour on the street than I usually sell in a whole day in my restaurant. I have got all my family working frantically in the kitchen cooking more curry. We must make hay while the sun shines."

"Yes, well I'm glad somebody's making something out of it. I'm certainly not. I've already missed my pre-match drink with Sir Edward in the Bar." He put the white plastic fork into the curry that was packed in a cardboard lunchbox. Then he took a bite. "Delicious! I must say you make a jolly fine curry. Here's five pounds. Keep the change. By the way, you don't know anyone reliable who could sit here in my car while I go to the match? I don't feel like just deserting it in case they manage to clear the traffic in the next hour or two."

"I hope that doesn't happen, sir. It would be very bad for my business."

"Yes, well I don't want to be responsible for causing even more congestion. Whoever sits in it can just park it in the nearest space and wait for me."

"My second cousin has just arrived from India with his family and is staying with me. He is a high caste Brahmin and a man of the highest integrity. I shall tell him to come and sit here

36

while you are gone. He would be only too happy to oblige such a fine sahib. Unfortunately it is not everyone who would entrust their car to an Indian."

"What nonsense! I had a couple of grooms to attend my horses all the time I was in India. Most loyal chaps in the world. I still send them a tenner every Christmas. I'll give your man five pounds for his trouble."

The second cousin arrived a few minutes later and the colonel gave him his instructions and showed him the gears. Then he buttoned up his tweed coat, put on his gloves and joined the happy throng of rugby patrons who were singing bawdy songs as they made their way along the footpath. Every few steps they took a swig of whisky from their hip flasks — "to warm the innards" as they said — and, by the time they reached the token anti-apartheid protest outside the ground, they were all in the highest of spirits.

"But apartheid's coming to an end!" they roared at the pathetic looking crowd of about three dozen stalwarts who were standing there with placards.

"It doesn't matter. There is still injustice in the world and, while it lasts, no none should be allowed to play rugby," screamed back the black bishop who, as group leader, was desperately trying to keep the dying movement alive so that he could continue travelling all round the world — First Class — to address meetings of gullible supporters who gave him large sums of money. He was surrounded by several clergymen with effeminate voices, a couple of sad looking students and a bunch of hairy legged monsters from a local feminists' co-operative who looked as if they should have been playing in the British team and giving extra weight to the scrum.

"Well I must say the bishop looks even worse in the flesh than he does on television," guffawed Colonel Byng-Moresby. "I don't see the point of winning all the World Wars for freedom just to have a cheeky native like that come over here and tell us which rugger matches we can go to and which ones we can't."

37

"Yes, I wouldn't like to meet him in a lonely lane on a dark night," giggled the girl who was walking behind him. "You never know what he might do to you. I'd far rather meet the Springbok captain. Ooh, he's so gorgeous! I've had his photo on my bedroom wall for weeks."

After the bawling of the bishop the next sound to assail their ears was the slang of the touts. "Any tickets to sell? Or buy? Special prices for such a chaotic day! Not to mention it being the Match of the Century."

"I'll bet they're doing a roaring trade to-day," said the girl with the Springbok on her wall.

"Yes, but only the ones who managed to get here," replied Byng-Moresby. "Those who live a long way away might find that they drew the short straw. Loads of tickets but no buyers. Ha! Ha! Ha! Serves them right. Too clever by half if you ask me."

One of the unfortunately absent purveyors of tickets was Barney Barlow who derived his income by taking advantage of the British public's insatiable appetite for grand events at which he handed out tickets to people with fat wallets at prices that always gave him a fat profit. His circuit consisted of Wimbledon, Lords, Wembley, Twickenham and the theatres of Shaftesbury Avenue.

He spent his entire life savings on buying ninety-six rugby tickets for the big match. Despite several good offers during the past week he had refrained from selling them in the belief — borne out by years of experience — that the longer he left them, the more money people were prepared to pay.

Barney had never before had so many tickets for one event; so, to celebrate his imminent fortune, he spent most of Friday night in his local getting exceedingly drunk. On credit. He had outlaid everything on the tickets and was left with only the Tube fare to Twickenham. "I'll pay you to-morrow night," he said to the rotund publican as he sat on the high stool at the bar guzzling pints of Worthington's Bitter .

"And what security might you have to offer for this outstanding loan?"

"These!" crowed Barney as he pulled out the wad of tickets from his inside pocket. "As good as the Bank of England. Worth more than twenty thousand pounds. And no tax!"

■

When he woke up at ten on Saturday morning Barney could feel the effects of a mild hangover from his night of drinking. He got up, showered and had breakfast. Then he made his way to the Woodford Underground Station for a leisurely ride to Twickenham.

He was more than a little annoyed when he found that the station was closed. There was a handwritten notice hanging from the metal grill across the station entrance. It stated that all services were cancelled until further notice due to a strike by drivers and guards.

Barney looked around for a taxi but there wasn't one. So he rang for a mini-cab. Half a hour later a white Vauxhall from the mini-cab company pulled up and the driver asked him where he wanted to go.

"Twickenham."

"What? To-day?"

"Yes, of course."

"Not to-day. Maybe to-morrow."

"But to-morrow will be too late."

"Try chartering a helicopter."

"What's going on?"

"I've just come from the West End and the whole area is clogged with traffic. Every bridge across the Thames has been blocked by the authorities — I mean, the councillors. And the tunnels too. Nothing is moving. And no way am I going back into it. Now if you want to go to Watford, that's a different matter. I'm prepared to drive you there; the traffic won't be up that far."

"I said 'Twickenham' — not 'Watford'! Now, listen: if you

can get me to Twickenham I'll give you a free ticket to the match. They're as scarce as hen's teeth."

"What match?"

"The rugby test between the Springboks and the British Lions. Biggest match of the century!"

"Sorry, mate. Soccer's my game. I wouldn't know one end of a rugby pitch from another. It'd be a complete waste. Now, if you were to give me a ticket to the Watford match, that'd be different."

Barney had difficulty keeping his cool. "If you can't drive me all the way to Twickenham, how far are you prepared to go before we reach the traffic jam?"

"Hard to say, really, but we'll give it a go. Probably get as far as Highbury or Islington."

"Okay. Let's go."

"Just one thing."

"What?"

"We've had so many bad debts lately that it's now company policy to ask for the fare in advance. Let's see......Highbury..... Ten pounds plus ten pounds for calling me out. If it's any more I'll stop at Highbury and ask you for some extra bread."

"Hell, I've only got the Tube fare. Three pounds. But see these tickets....." He pulled out the bundle from his coat pocket. "They're worth twenty thousand ...... if I can get to the ground and sell them. For God's sake, man, I'll write down my address and you can come round to-night and I'll give you both the fare and a hundred pound tip."

"Sorry, guv. I've heard that one before. In fact, nearly every day. And anyway, from what I've seen of the traffic you won't be able to get to Twickenham at all to-day. So how are you going to realise that sort of money? Can't see anyone on this side of the river giving you three hundred quid for a ticket to a match way the hell on the other side of London that they can't get to. Try walking. You should get there before next season." He pressed his foot on the accelerator and roared off.

40

Barney set off in a south-westerly direction. He looked at his watch; it was twenty past eleven. He went to turn on his transistor but remembered that he had left it on the kitchen table. And there was no time to go back for it.

A quarter of an hour later he saw a black cab coming towards him; it was showing its yellow light. He ran out on the road and flagged it down.

By a circuitous route they managed to finish up in Hornsey at ten minutes to one but could get no further because of the bank-up of cars in all directions.

"I am at Hornsey," screamed the driver into his radio tele-phone. "How the hell can I get from here to the south-west without getting in the jam?"

"You can't," said Control. "There's a tail-back from where you are all the way down to the West End. And even the City."

"Cor blimey! Why is it so thick up here? We're miles from the blocked bridges."

"Yes, but not from Camden Lock."

"I didn't know there was a bridge across Camden Lock. Last time I was there I saw people jumping across it."

"No, the problem is the big Saturday market there. It's bad every Saturday but to-day it's worse than ever. Traffic is banked up in all directions from the market and the line that you're in up at Hornsey is part of the Camden Market jam as opposed to the blocked bridges jam, the Wembley jam, the Twickenham jam and all the other jams which have now become one big jam."

"And what's that called?"

"The London United jam."

"Who's the patron of that? Prince Philip?"

"No, the Mad Hatter."

"Sorry, guv," said the driver as he turned to Barney. "This is the end of the line. Fare please. Three pounds."

Barney handed him the three coins; it was the last of his money.

"And what about a tip for the driver?"

"Can't."

"Cunning bit o' scum!"

Still with his bunch of tickets that were fast becoming worthless, Barney started walking along Tottenham Lane, up Crouch End Hill and along Hornsey Lane. The air was filled with a combination of honking horns and loud car stereos. "It's like the end of the world," he thought dismally as he went past hundreds of cars that were bumper to bumper and not going anywhere.

When he reached the high bridge across Archway he paused to catch his breath. Although he spent half his life outside sports grounds he was anything but sportsmanlike fit himself. From the bridge he stared down in wonder at the long lines of stationary traffic that extended both up and down the wide Archway Road. He looked at his watch. It was twenty to two. And the match was due to start at 2.30. He knew that, even in normal traffic conditions, it would be impossible to drive from Archway to Twickenham in fifty minutes.

He pulled out the wad of useless tickets and flicked through them. Then he calculated how much they had cost him. Eight thousand, four hundred pounds! His entire life savings.

He climbed up on to the parapet of the high bridge and looked down. A split second later he was shooting head first through the crisp afternoon air in the direction of the road three hundred feet below. He landed on the shiny red roof of a Lamborghini.

"What was that?" exclaimed the passenger, Henrietta Harrington-Hoot who was all dressed up and on her way to a wedding with her husband, Hugo.

"Could be anything on a crazy day like this," he replied drily. "Probably a spaceman who lost his spaceship. Perhaps there's traffic congestion up there too."

"Ooh, look! The red paint on the roof is melting. See, it's starting to trickle down the windscreen," exclaimed the astounded wife. But Hugo wasn't looking. His attention was centred on the driver's side window through which he could see a steady fall of priceless rugby tickets fluttering to the ground.

"It's raining! " he said to his wife.

"Where? I can't see any water on the window."

"No, it's not raining water."

"What's is raining then?"

"Rugger tickets."

Hugo rang the nearby Whittington Hospital on his car 'phone and reported that there was some unknown creature on his roof which might once have been a human being and he wanted it removed as quickly as possible. Then he rang the nearby petrol station and asked them to send a boy down with a bucket of water and sponge to wash the unsightly blood off the windscreen.

"Don't wind your window down for a while," he said to Henrietta.

"Why not?"

"Because ticket touts have a bad smell about them. I don't want it to get inside the car."

Had Barney remembered to take his transistor with him he would never have jumped. Indeed, after the 1.30 News there was a special announcement that the match was being postponed for an hour because four of the British players were still trying to get through the traffic.

When this announcement was made over the loud speakers at Twickenham there was a rush of eager supporters to the Lions' changing room. The coach was inundated with drunken offers to fill the breach. These doughty volunteers included social players, ex-England trialists, programme sellers and one old gezeer on a walking-stick who claimed that he had just missed being selected for the Lions in 1953 and never imagined that his chance might come again.

One balding, over-weight North London car dealer actually got down on his hands and knees, crawled between the coach's legs, stripped off in the dressing room, grabbed the nearest jock-strap, shorts and jersey and then, with the greatest of effort, began doing push-ups on the cold concrete floor. Weighing in at nineteen and a half stone, he claimed he could add no end of weight to the scrum and was just what was needed "to push those bloody Boers all the way back to South Africa". When he was told that the missing players had at last been located and would be at the ground in twenty minutes he sat down on the wooden bench and blubbered like a baby.

While all this was going on inside the dressing room the crowds in the stands were being entertained by a Highland Pipe Band and marching girls. However, the highlight of the afternoon was when a well-formed young lady in the front row of seats took off all her clothes and streaked across the grass to the other side where she was eagerly grabbed by a couple of lesbian policewomen.

The two dikes took her to a small cell-like room under the Stand where they snapped her photograph from various angles and took down the details of her name, address, measurements and telephone number. These particulars were later placed on the notice board in the Women's Room at the police station with the result that the poor streaker was hounded by indecent telephone calls for next six months.

The delay in starting the match meant that the tickets which dropped on to Archway Road along with their owner were not entirely valueless. Although the very correct and particular Hugo was reluctant to get out of his car and breathe the same air as a dead ticket tout, other members of the public had no such qualms. In particular, one Max Heatherwick, who was riding up Archway Road towards his bed-sitter after purchasing a new head-lamp for his motor-bike at the garage down the road.

The proprietor of the garage had had his radio on at full volume and Max, a keen rugger supporter from Bath who was studying architecture in London, had heard the statement that the match had been postponed for an hour. "Good," he thought, "that 'll give me time to get home and roll a couple of joints and I won't miss the first few minutes of it on the box like I thought I would." If Max had had any choice in the matter he would have been there himself but it was nearly the end of term and his student grant just didn't stretch that far.

As he drove up Archway Road he saw the last few feet of Barney's fall and the subsequent landing on the roof of the Lamborghini. He slowed down and brought his machine to a halt beside the driver's window of the highly polished car.

Amazed at the well-dressed driver's *sang froid* he looked up towards the mess on the roof to see if there was anything he could do to help. On the way his eyes caught sight of the trail of fluttering tickets that were emanating from the torn pocket of the dead man's jacket. Max knelt down on the asphalt to see what they were. "Sacred Springboks!" he gasped as he read the small black print. He looked at his watch. It was 1.44 p.m. He recalled the radio announcement that the game had been postponed for an hour and then he calculated how long it would take to drive to Twickenham on the motor-bike.

Max had been living in London for three years during which time he had always had a motor-bike as well as girl-friends in most parts of the metropolis. He knew all the side roads and short-cuts and reasoned that, even with the unprecedented traffic, he could dodge and weave his way to Twickenham in seventy minutes.

He picked up a pile of about eighty tickets and went to get back on his bike. As he did so his eyes caught sight of Hugo whose expression had now turned to one of disdain. The driver just couldn't understand how anyone could be so low as to kneel down on a stony road and pick up rugby tickets that had been fingered by a ticket tout.

"I really don't know what the world's coming to!" he said to his over-dressed wife.

"Oh, come on. Don't be such a snob," she replied. "After all, we live in a free enterprise system and it's all a matter of supply and demand. Sellers and buyers. I can't see that being a ticket tout is much different from the way that you buy and sell shares for your clients in the City."

"True. I agree that the economic principle is the same. It's just that I don't like to see people from that class making money. Hell, if a chap like that sold enough tickets over the years he might one day be able to afford a Lamborghini."

"I see what you mean. On second thoughts it's a good thing that he's dead."

Max reached the gates of Twickenham half an hour before the start of the match. Barney wasn't the only ticket scalp not to have reached the venue with the result that prices were extremely healthy. However, in view of the short time remaining, Max decided not to be too greedy. But he still finished up with seven thousand pounds in his pocket — more than his entire year's student grant.

He kept the last ticket for himself. The two burly captains were just leading their teams on to the field as he climbed the concrete steps and took his seat above the half-way line.

Chapter Four

At Downing Street Mrs. Thatcher had been up since five. There were Foreign Office cables to read, a new Education Act to peruse, ministerial memoranda and a letter from the Governor of Hong Kong asking if he should pull the plug on the colony now or wait until 1997. Then she had to read the briefing papers for her afternoon meeting with the French President at Chequers. She chose a red, white and blue outfit which, she reflected, being the colours of both Britain and France, would be doubly appropriate. She knew that she had to make every post a winning post in order to gain access to the much needed French base at Djibouti. It was to be the key in the coming battle against the latest Moslem maniac and his primitive, ignorant followers.

It was just before twelve when she said good-bye to her husband, who was off to Twickenham with his cronies, and climbed into her car for the drive to Chequers in the tranquil Buckinghamshire countryside. She made the same journey most weekends and knew that, with her police escort, it never took more than an hour and a half.

"Good," she thought, "that will give me half an hour to spare before the President's helicopter arrives and I'll be able to see that everything is properly organised." But when they drove through the great iron gates of Downing Street they found that Whitehall was clogged with several lanes of extremely slow moving vehicles.

The Prime Minister had heard on the News that the councils were blocking the bridges but she never thought that it would be this bad. "See all these cars that are hardly moving," she said to her chauffeur. "That's what it'll be like if we ever get a Labour Government. Not just the occasional Saturday but every day." The little man duly expressed his horror at such a prospect and then accelerated a little as he found a gap between a couple of slow moving lanes.

It was twenty past twelve before they reached Trafalgar Square. The Prime Minister looked up at the statue of Nelson standing atop his high column and she reflected on his stirring words on the eve of battle. "Maybe I should have made a similar plea to the train drivers," she thought. "England expects every train driver to get his train in on time so that the passengers can get to the football." No, it didn't sound right.

The car came to a complete halt in Regent Street beside a busload of Japanese schoolchildren who recognised the Prime Minister, clapped politely and then started chanting, "England, England, Margaret Teacher. Margaret Teacher, Number One."

It was seven minutes to one before they reached the Marylebone Road and the Prime Minister worked out that she would have made faster progress if she had set out on foot. She now realised that she would never get to Chequers in time to greet the French President. Furthermore, if the reports on the car radio of a complete jam on the Westway Flyover were true, then she would be lucky to reach Buckinghamshire by nightfall. She called Downing Street on the car 'phone and spoke to her Private Secretary.

"Can't you get me a helicopter? We could turn into the Regent's Park and you could arrange one to collect me there."

"I'm sorry but we've already thought of that and there's not a helicopter we can lay our hands on. They're all out on charter to the B.B.C. and the newspapers who are up in the air taking photos of all the chaos down below."

"Well, what about the police choppers?"

"They're all in the air monitoring the situation and trying to ascertain the points of worst congestion. And now some of them have to escort the Queen's helicopter which is just leaving the grounds of Buckingham Palace to take Her Majesty and His Royal Highness to Twickenham for the rugby."

She put down the 'phone and looked at her watch. It was now one o'clock. "Oh, this is terrible," she thought as she dialled Chequers to ask if the Foreign Secretary had arrived. "At least *he'll* be able to deputise for me until I get through all this wretched traffic." But when she spoke to Chequers she was told that the Foreign Secretary had just rung to say that he was caught in the jam around the Wembley turn-off and didn't know when or even if he would ever reach Chequers.

She dialled Downing Street again and asked the secretary to find some local grandee who could perform the welcoming honours. "What about the Lord Lieutenant of Buckinghamshire?" she asked.

"I've already tried him and his daughter said that he's gone to the rugby match."

"Well what about the Duke of Buckingham? Isn't there a Duke of Buckingham?"

"Not any longer. The title has been extinct for more than a hundred years."

"Oh, this is terrible!" she screamed. "You know how touchy the French are. My task was going to be hard enough as it was without all this nonsense. Anyway, who have we got at Chequers at the moment who could step out to greet the President and his wife when their helicopter arrives on the lawn?"

"I have just ascertained that there is the cook, two house-maids, four gardeners and the duty policeman. I think the cook would be the best. He once worked in a restaurant in Paris and so presumably knows a bit of the lingo."

The Prime Minister put down the 'phone and turned to the security officer who was sitting alongside her. "If I don't get to Chequers within the hour all hell is going to break loose. The French will say that they've been insulted, they won't let us use their base, we'll have to operate with longer lines of supply which

49

means we'll lose more 'planes and more pilots. Valuable British lives will be lost if I don't get to Chequers by two o'clock. What about a police motor-cycle?"

"You mean you'll ride a motor-bike?" asked the man in dismay.

"No, I don't know how to operate them but I don't mind riding pillion." But there were no police motor-bikes for miles. All the cops were deployed at the football grounds and at Twickenham where they were happily getting ready to watch their favourite teams under the pretext of controlling the crowds.

Above the sound of honking horns came a loud roar. Distant at first, it grew to a mighty crescendo as the Hell's Angels roared along the footpath in close formation.

"What's that? Messerschmitts? Junkers?" cried Mrs Thatcher. "Don't say I'm going to have to fight another Battle of Britain as well."

"No," replied the security officer. "I think it's just the Hell's Angels out for their Saturday ride. They should all be in jail if you ask me."

"Well at least they're going places. More than we are," she said with her usual clarity of thought.

The Prime Minister had at last had enough of the incompetence with which she seemed to be surrounded. She opened the car door and stepped out.

Five of the Angels had already sped past when she alighted. She tried to flag down the sixth one but he recognised her, pulled a face and roared ahead. When Myles rode up in Position Number Seven she waved her handbag in his direction. He slowed down and veered into a gap so as to avoid a collision with the bike behind him.

"What is it?" he asked in his polished public school accent as he switched off his machine and removed the crash helmet from his head. The Prime Minister was momentarily taken aback. She looked at his face; it was tender, friendly, clean-shaven. Not at all what she had expected.

"Young man!" she said. "Could you please drive me to Chequers. We're not getting anywhere in this traffic. It's all because of those dreadful councils blocking the bridges."

"Oh, I don't think the bridge traffic reaches up this far," replied Myles. "We're now into the football traffic. To be fair, I'd say that the demarcation line is about half a mile further back."

"It is a matter of great national importance that I get to Chequers as soon as possible. It is important for Britain, for our American ally, for the world."

"I don't think that my job instructions allow you to drive off with a strange and unknown man on a motor-bike," put in the officious security officer. *"Especially a Hell's Angel."*

"Well at the moment he's a jolly sight more use to me than all the rest of you. I'll make my own decision for my security this afternoon, thank-you very much." She turned to Myles and asked him one simple question. "And are you one of us?"

"Well, yes. I suppose I am. I've always voted Tory."

"And what is your job when you're not riding motor-bikes?"

"I'm a barrister."

"A barrister! And what does your head of chambers think of your extra-curricular activities?"

"I am the head of chambers."

"What?"

"You see, in our chambers we take it in turns to be head. A week about. Saves all the bowing and scraping that goes on in other chambers. And it's my turn this week."

"Well I'm glad that we don't follow that system in Cabinet. Think of all the terrible things that would happen if I ever let any of my ministers put their hands on the rudder of the nation."

"Yes, well if you come on my bike you'll have to wear a crash helmet. It's the law, I'm afraid."

"But what about my hairdo?"

"It'll be worse if the wind blows it around."

By now several other Angels had stopped and were witnessing the amazing conversation between their brother, Myles, and

51

the Prime Minister of Great Britain. They looked a fearsome lot but Mrs Thatcher was not afraid; fear was not and never had been any part of her make-up.

"'Ere, Maggie, wear mine," offered Dead Eye Dick. He held out the helmet in his oil-stained hand. "Just make sure you sign it before you hand it back to Myles. I'll be able to auction it at Sothebys when you die. Get back some of the tax I've paid."

The Prime Minister put on the helmet, climbed on the back of Myles' Sportster and instructed the driver to go as fast as he could. She held on tight around his waist and he could feel the clip of the handbag digging into his back.

Progress was slow at first but, after they cleared the bottleneck at theWembley turn-off, he pressed the accelerator hard and,by the time they reached the edge of London, they were travelling at a speed of a hundred and twenty miles an hour. On they went — past rolling meadows, thatched farmhouses, silent churchyards and endless hedges of hawthorn. With her features partially covered by the full faced helmet the Prime Minister was unrecognised by those whom they passed. In fact she was not recognised until they roared up the main drive of Chequers at twenty minutes past two. And the first one to identify her was the sharp eyed President of France.

He and his stylishly dressed wife had alighted from their helicopter at two o'clock as planned and he was more than a little annoyed at the welcoming party that was lined up to greet him. The cook was there in his high white hat and so were the two housemaids in their starched white uniforms and lace bonnets. One of the gardeners had been a boy seaman in the Navy during the War and seemed to remember that when officers got married everyone held up their swords. So he issued garden spades to his colleagues and all four of them stood in line with their spades raised in the form of an arch. The duty policeman saluted, the President saluted back, the policeman returned the salute and then asked the Frenchman to sign his notebook.

The cook explained in his best French that the Prime

Minister, the Foreign Secretary and all the other secretaries were caught in the traffic and no one had any idea when they would arrive. "Maybe for dinner, but maybe not for dinner," he kept saying.

"And what is it that has blocked all the roads?" asked the President.

"Traffic for the football. Too many football supporters."

"*Mon Dieu!* The English and their football!"

It was at this moment that they heard a tremendous roar of machinery coming up the Victory Drive. They looked out at the stately, beech lined avenue and saw a motor-bike approaching at great speed.

The first thing the President saw was the white skull and crossbones painted on the front of Myles' black leather jacket. Then he recognised the face of the pillion passenger.

"I don't believe it!" he exclaimed to his wife. "You never know what that woman is going to do next. The English are obviously not as strait-laced as they like us to think."

"What do you mean?"

"Who would have believed it possible that the Madame Thatcher would have *une affaire* with a gigolo? Oh, you can never trust women! Not even a Prime Minister. The moment that Monsieur Dennis turns his back to go to the rugby — bang! — she jumps on a motor-bike and goes riding through the countryside with a toy-boy. I thought that it would only be a French Prime Minister who would have the spunk and style to do such a thing but I am humbly mistaken. It must be an affair of great passion for do you see how tightly she is holding him around his waist? I must reappraise my opinion of her. She is a truly remarkable lady. I think that our talks will go very well for I have a new respect for her."

"Mister President, I hope you haven't been waiting long," she said as she climbed off the bike, removed the crash helmet and walked up to greet her guest. There wasn't a hair out of place or a crease in her clothing.

"And thank-you, Myles," she said. "Cook will get you some afternoon tea."

∎

Among the witnesses to the Prime Minister's flagging down of Myles were the occupants of an ambulance that was travelling in the opposite direction. The driver was more than a little frustrated. It was not that he had a desperately ill or dying patient in the vehicle; on the contrary, it was only a broken arm which, although painful, was not exactly life endangering.

The elderly female patient, who had been sitting on the front seat next to him for the past four hours, was a Carmelite nun from the Convent of Saint Clare which was situated in the beautiful Berkshire countryside some forty miles west of London. It was a closed order of sisters in which the vow of Silence was absolute; it made no allowances for ambulances, hospitals and traffic jams. And so for once the normally talkative Cockney driver was unable to chat to his passenger.

It was the first time that the ninety-eight year old nun had been outside the gates of her cloistered home since she joined the convent as a sixteen year old novice in 1908. Her whole life had been one of spiritual contemplation and total isolation from the world and all its many troubles. She had never had to worry about mortgages, childbirth, relationships, divorce, money matters and all the other myriad problems that are the lot of ordinary mortals. Which, of course, was why she had lived so long.

Even the World Wars had passed her by. She could remember hearing the guns of the Somme as their droning sound carried across the Channel in 1916. That is, until the Mother Superior got up and closed all the windows. Then in 1940 she and her silent friends had seen a few stray Heinkels flying over Berkshire but it was nothing to worry about; most of the bombs were being dropped on London - away to the east - and the Midlands in the north. In any case, the nuns had dug a trench in their vegetable garden and, if that didn't save them, well it was obviously time for

God to take them to their heavenly reward. It would be the fulfilment of all their dreams. But God chose to leave them on Earth a little longer which was why Sister Constance had now been sitting in a traffic jam for four hours.

She had seen cars before. Big black square ones with running boards and canvas hoods and spare tyres strapped across their boots. She could remember the drivers in big leather gloves and goggles, cranking them to start their motors.

She had even seen a traffic jam. In the high street of her childhood village in Hereford. One of the first Rolls Royces had collided with a big horse drawn cart that was loaded with fresh vegetables. The whole high street had been blocked for two hours and nothing could get past. There were two cars and three drays drawn by horses banked up in one direction and a coach and four going the other way. Sister Constance could even remember the date; it was the King's Birthday week-end in 1906. And that was the only traffic jam that she had ever seen. Until to-day.

Her vow of silence prevented her from asking the driver if the traffic was always like this or even if they would ever get out of it. All she wanted to do was to get back to the peace and order of the convent.

When Mrs. Thatcher jumped out of the car and started waving her handbag at the rough looking motor cyclists, Sister Constance gave the ambulance driver a quizzical look. In her genteel eyes it didn't seem a very ladylike thing to do.

"That's the bloody Prime Minister!" said the driver.

Sister Constance looked horrified. She began to wonder why God had sent her so many problems all at once: first the broken arm, then the traffic jam and now a driver who is either drunk or mad because he can't even distinguish a Prime Minister from a Prime Minister's wife.

She could remember seeing photographs in ladies' magazines of the Prime Minister's wife and took a closer look at the features of the woman who was waving the handbag. "No, it's definitely not Asquith's wife," she concluded. "Or even Asquith's mistress." Then she realised that old Asquith would probably be dead by now and that they would have a new Prime Minister.

She leaned towards the middle of the seat and took a surreptitious sniff. No, she couldn't smell alcohol; therefore the man must be mad. Perhaps an escapee from Bedlam who had hijacked the ambulance. She knew that there was only one way out of her multiple dilemma. "Oh, God, please come and take me NOW!" she begged her Maker under her breath. But God decided to leave her there. In the traffic jam.

Chapter Five

So great and sudden was the jam that the transport authorities in London were at a loss to know what to do. Eventually they decided that they needed some firm direction from "Above". And so they tried to contact the Secretary of State for Transport who was spending the week-end at his country seat in north Devon.

"He's gone out," said his wife who was annoyed at being disturbed in her garden.

"Where is he?"

"At the golf club. Where he always is on a Saturday morning. And I know that he doesn't like to be disturbed. Here's the number."

By the time that the call was made to the golf club Humphrey Granville-Gore, the tall, distinguished looking Secretary of State for Transport in Her Majesty's Government, was five strokes ahead of his opponent on the fourteenth hole and was putting for a birdie. He was enjoying his morning and was more than a little surprised to see the club captain running from the clubhouse waving a putter and a Number One wooden club in the air. "Old Willoughby must have at last flipped his lid," observed Humphrey. "Always thought that that woman would prove too much for him."

"Is he her fourth husband or her fifth?" asked his opponent who was just picking himself up after falling down in the sandy bunker.

"The sixth. And they were all called 'Charlie'. One of them used to be my bank manager. A right royal bastard he was too. I've had to blackball him from three clubs."

Humphrey Granville-Gore sank his ball in the hole. As he bent down to retrieve it he could hear his name being called in the distance by the wildly waving club captain. "Mister Granville-Gore, sir."

"Clubhouse must have caught on fire, he's in such a state," chortled Humphrey. "What is it?" he called through the silence and crispness of the morning.

"Telephone for you, sir. It's urgent."

"What's happened? Has war been declared?"

"No, there's a traffic jam in London and they want you to give some directions."

"Can't you see that I'm in the middle of a very important golf match?"

"Yes, sir, but they said that you must come immediately."

"A traffic jam in London!" exclaimed Humphrey to his equally surprised opponent. "There are always traffic jams in London. Every day. Bloody nerve they've got to interrupt me in the middle of a golf match." He turned to the club captain and said, "Take the number and tell them that I'll call back when I've finished the round. There are only four more holes to play."

"Very well, sir, but don't say that I didn't warn you."

"Mrs. Willoughby hasn't been getting at you again, has she?"

"No, sir. She's up in Scotland with her grandchildren. Half term."

Humphrey teed up at the fifteenth and hit a nice long drive down the fairway. His opponent's ball went into the rough.

"The cheek of it, Gerald. Placing a long distance call to Devon just to remind me that there's the usual Saturday morning traffic jam in London. I can't stand people who panic."

When the two golfers finally finished their round Humphrey walked over to the Secretary's Office to put in his card. Then he ambled across to the 'phone by the bar and made a collect call to his office in Whitehall.

"What the hell's going on up there?" he asked. "Have you

58

all lost your heads or something?"

"No, but you might lose your's when Parliament starts debating this thing on Tuesday."

"What thing?"

"The whole of London is trapped in a traffic jam and no one seems able to unjam it. That's why we rang you. To get some directions."

"Very well then, I want you to do three things. First, ring the church bells. All over London. That'll warn the people that there's a traffic jam and, if they've got any sense, they'll all stay indoors and watch their television sets. Match of the Day will be on in a couple of hours.

Secondly, get the B.B.C. to make radio announcements every ten minutes telling the people to leave their cars at home and to travel by Tube."

"But there's no Underground. They've all gone on strike for the day."

"Oh, well, tell them to walk. Do them good on a crisp day like this."

"Very well, sir, and what's your third direction?"

"Third thing? Oh yes, I remember. Tell them to light a big fire at the top of Hampstead Heath. We always do that in times of crisis. Like during the Armada when we were all wondering whether the Spaniards would land. The Heath is high enough to be seen from most points in London and, when everyone sees the fire, they'll know that it's a warning — that something's wrong. So they'll turn on their radios and will learn of the traffic jam. Then, if they've got any sense, they'll leave their cars at home. I think that if you follow those three directions the situation should eventually resolve itself."

"Yes, sir," said the young secretary in Whitehall as he shook his head and wondered if he'd be getting a new Secretary of State for Transport in the next Cabinet reshuffle.

After he put down the 'phone the Honourable Humphrey Granville-Gore joined his opponent at the bar for a little bit of nineteenth hole liquid refreshment. The steward handed him his usual drinking vessel which was overflowing with cold, frothy lager. He always drank out of the same mug which was, in fact, the skull of his great-grandfather, Bishop Granville-Gore, who had been a missionary in Fiji before he was put into the cooking pot and eaten by the local cannibals as "roasted missionary". The skull had been presented to the Transport Secretary during his ministerial visit to the South Sea Islands in 1988 by a Fijian chief who proudly claimed to be the grandson of the chief cook at the earlier ceremony. "My grandfather, he always say 'Granville-Gore flesh — very tasty — but his boots very tough'," were the words that the savage spoke as he dropped the thing into Humphrey's outstretched hands.

At a loss to know what to do with it Humphrey had had the orifices plugged and then had the thing hollowed out and mounted on a silver base with an ivory handle going out from where the left ear had once been. His wife had refused to have it in the house so he kept it at the golf club where he had used it so many times that the skull had long since turned pure white from regular washing.

"You know, Gerald, there really is some huge traffic jam up in London. Worse than usual. But I've issued instructions on how to deal with it."

"Good. But it's none of our concern. We're miles away from it down here."

"True. But they'll probably blame it all on me."

"In God's name why? You've been playing golf all the morning. I can vouch for that. I'd even go to court for you and swear it on the Bible. You've got an unanswerable alibi."

"Yes, but they'll say that I should have built more roads."

"And should you?"

"Probably — but it's not as easy as it sounds. Every time that I've proposed a new road or motorway or by-pass or flyover to alleviate the traffic I've been faced with the most amazing obstructions by the locals. Sometimes even violence." He pulled the leg of his plus fours out from his stocking to show a scar on his shin where he had been struck with a horse-whip by a mad spinster in Kensington.

"The moment that I try to do something to aid the flow of traffic they organise protest meetings, motorway marches, burn my effigy on every village common and send hate mail through the post.. One of them even stood up at a meeting and accused me of being a cross between Hitler and Speer because they reckoned that I was trying to create a new Fourth Reich by destroying their homes.

And then, when I made the eminently sensible suggestion to build fast-flow tunnels under Hyde Park and Regent's Park, I came up against the greenies. 'No,' they screamed, 'the vibrations might harm the root growth of the trees.' Then the animal liberationists came in on the side of the worms and accused me of deliberately trying to upset the balance of nature by threatening the habitat of the earthworm. They'd rather spend their lives sitting in traffic jams then upset an earthworm.

And it's not just the chattering classes of the Left who scream and yell. Some of the most dogged resistance has come right from the heart of the Conservative Party — the hunting crowd who don't want concrete motorways on the land where they chase the fox."

"Don't blame them!"

"I tell you, Gerald, every single proposal I have made has faced this sort of opposition. Which, of course, is why I haven't been able to build any new roads.

As you know, every year there are hundreds of thousands of extra vehicles being driven and yet the roads remain much the same as they were in the eighteenth century. Now with all this chaos in London, the newspapers and all the other professional troublemakers will blame me for not building any new roads. Believe me, Gerald, it hasn't been for lack of trying. Some of my predecessors' proposals have been bogged down in planning tribunals for more than twenty years. There are some lawyers who have spent their whole careers on the same road case.

The only thing that I've been able to achieve in all my years as Her Majesty's Secretary of State for Transport is the replacement of all the motorway signs on the M4. And the struggle to get them through just about killed me."

"Why? Who on earth would object to new motorway signs?"

"Oh, you'd be surprised! It took two years just to decide on the colour. Blue or green background. The Tories all wanted blue while the environmentalists insisted that they be green so as to tone in with the trees."

"So what colour did you finish up with?"

"Well, one side called it 'bluish green' while the other mob insisted that it was 'greenish blue'. There was just as big a row over the colour of the lettering. The Safety Brigade wanted luminous white so that they could be seen clearly in the dark but the environmentalists argued that, if they were too bright, they would upset the owls who might not be able to breed properly. Their reasoning went that an owl who was temporarily blinded by a bright sign might not be able to see if its prospective mating partner was male or female and therefore there was a great danger that the owl population would turn homosexual. I was even accused in the papers of promoting homosexuality. And of being one.

After a year of this ridiculous wrangling over the *colour* of the lettering we then came to the problem of how big the letters should be. I wanted them to be large enough for the average motorist to be able to see — which, after all, is the whole purpose of signs. But the blind lobby insisted that they be at least double that size so that they could be read by the partially blind.

When I pointed out that the partially blind should not be driving cars on busy highways I was told that, although the partially blind don't drive, they should not be deprived of the opportunity of being a navigator for a sighted driver. One of them even squirted acid in my eyes to try to make me blind so that I would *see* their point of view.

So I agreed to an enlargement of the lettering and then found that I had upset the security people. 'If the letters were that big,' they argued, 'the signs could be read from enemy satellites' that are apparently orbiting the earth and taking photos of us all down here in Britain."

"Do you think they would have got a shot of that last putt I did on the eighteenth hole? I wouldn't mind getting a copy of it."

"God only knows! And do you know what the biggest argument was over?"

"No."

"The damned sticks that anchor the signposts into the ground. The safety lobby wanted rubber ones so that, if ever an errant driver crashed into one of them, he wouldn't be hurt. But an ex-servicemen's organisation insisted that they be made of wood so that they could be easily chopped down in the event of a Nazi invasion. Remember how we took all the signs down in 1940 to confuse the Germans if they landed. I tried to point out to them that times have changed but they fought me to the bitter end. Seemed to regard it as their last great campaign.

And, since I've been able to build only signs and no roads, the papers will say that my bright new signs contributed to to-day's congestion by leading all the drivers into London whereas, with the old signs, a few hundred of them would have got lost in country lanes. It really is the most impossible situation."

"Yes, I'm glad I'm in carpets. Only thing I ever have to worry about is the price of wool."

"Mind you, this traffic jam will help our balance of payments figures. If nothing can move in London, then our petrol consumption will be down for the month; we won't have to buy so much petrol from abroad. Or rubber. After all, there won't be much wear and tear on the tyres to-day."

"Yes, I've always wondered about that."

"About what?"

"The stocks of rubber. You see, there are only so many rubber trees in Malaya and, if there's too great a demand for tyres....well...then there won't be enough rubber for the other things."

"What other things?"

"The things that we men buy in the chemist shop."

"Good God! I never thought of that. Perhaps we should ban cars altogether and go back to the horse."

■
———

The Chief Ranger at Hampstead Heath was somewhat surprised when he received a 'phone call from the Whitehall office of the Secretary of State for Transport. He was even more surprised when he was told to light a huge fire at the site of the old beacon near Whitestone Pond.

"At four hundred and forty-three feet it is the highest point in London and everyone will be able to see the flames," said the polished voice from Transport. "It is a personal order from the Secretary of State himself. A Queen's Messenger is on his way to you with written confirmation of the command."

The Chief Ranger was mystified. He knew that Whitestone Pond was the site of one of the chain of beacons that were lit in 1588 to warn the people of the approach of the Spanish Armada. Surely the little men from the Iberian Peninsula couldn't be on their way again. He had read that they wanted to get their greedy hands on Gibraltar but for one of Europe's most backward countries to have a crack at a nuclear super-power like Britain seemed a bit over the top. Even for a bunch of excitable Latins.

"Might I ask what is the purpose of this fire, sir?" he asked.

"Yes, there is a traffic jam. The fire will warn people not to take their cars out and add to the congestion."

The Chief Ranger could hear the honking horns of the impatient drivers as they waited in stationary lines all around the Heath. And now a hundred church bells were ringing out from the many spires that rose up from the well-heeled villages of Hampstead and Highgate.

"Very well, sir. We'll get a fire going straight away. Fortunately there are a lot of dead trees lying around up there. The ones that came down in the Great Storm in January. It'll be a good chance to get rid of them."

"The bigger the blaze the better; more people will see it. And the Secretary of State will be very pleased."

The Chief Ranger put down the receiver and picked up his two-way radio. "Hmmm," he thought, "at least it'll provide the rangers with a bit of variation. Be a change from counting squirrels and jumping out from behind bushes to tell young lovers to put their pants back on."

He sent out a message on his radio to summon all the other rangers who were scattered across the broad acres of the heath. He told them to gather at Whitestone Pond with as many cans of petrol as they could lay their hands on. The Chief then drove himself up to the site in a jeep; for the next hour they used the vehicle to drag huge dead trees towards the great combustible pile that was being formed in the middle of the grassy knoll. A few members of the public with pyromaniac tendencies lent a hand and a great air of expectation prevailed.

Soon all was ready and the Chief Ranger threw a burning branch of brushwood on to the petrol soaked trees. The flames shot up into the air and spread quickly. The Chief rubbed his hands in satisfaction. He knew that the fire would soon be seen from most parts of the city and that the Secretary of State and his minions would be more than happy.

The fire began to spread through the high grass that surrounded the area. "Let it burn!" cried one of the rangers. "Save us having to mow it next week. It won't go across the path."

The flames were moving in a northerly direction, being fanned by the gentle south wind that had been blowing all day. But the wind was getting stronger. And the flames did cross the path. They spread quickly on to the West Heath and soon the oaks and elms that had been standing for more than a hundred years were ablaze. The ever quickening breeze was carrying the flames from tree to tree.

The Chief Ranger contacted the Fire Brigade on his two-way radio but he knew it was a forlorn hope. The Fire Chief sadly informed him that, even if his engines could get out of the fire station—which they couldn't because it was blocked by a double-decker bus and three Leyland trucks that were all touching bumpers — there was no way that they could get through the blocked streets to the burning Heath.

The fire was now enveloping the Vale of Health, the East Heath and even the Sandy Heath. And it was not just the oaks and alders, the firs and silver birch that were being destroyed. Stately homes and their priceless contents were starting to burn in the now gale force winds. And also the wildlife. Charred squirrels and hedgehogs, rats and hares littered the blackened and burning ground.

There were several cases of coitus interruptus as teenage lovers ran out of bushes in various states of undress to escape the fast moving flames. A few ramblers and dog walkers formed a human chain to pass buckets of water from the ponds up to the fire but it was like a man putting up the palm of his hand to stop a gale.

The professional gentlefolk of Hampstead were not at all pleased with the thick pall of smoke that was passing over their village from the Heath. They rose from their oak and walnut writing desks and closed the windows lest the smoke might damage the expensive paintings that hung on the walls of their drawing rooms and dining rooms. Worse still, a spark might ignite some of the thousands of typewritten manuscripts that Hampstead people were forever submitting to their publishers. Some were steamy, some were sleazy, some historical, some philosophical, but all were written in Hampstead.

The fire had now spread to a row of shops near the Heath which housed a clockmaker, a tailor and a bookshop. The bookshop was so exclusive that it stocked only titles that had been written by Hampstead residents; and these covered three floors. The paperbacks burnt first, then the hard backs, then the wooden shelves and finally the building itself.

Several local authors died of shock when they heard about the destruction of the bookshop while the President of the Hampstead Residents' and Writers' Association declared it "the blackest day in the history of English literature; an equivalent disaster would have been if Shakespeare had fallen out of his pram and drowned in the Avon before he learned to write."

This provoked a counterclaim from the President of the Heath Protection Society who declared that the thousands of burnt oaks and elms were a greater loss to mankind than "a bloody bookshop". The ensuing debate filled the Letters to the Editor pages of the local newspaper, the Ham and High, for the next six months and led to several new manuscripts being written on the subject of the relative merits of trees and books.

The whole issue became extremely messy with the environmentalists charging that the thousands of charred tree trunks that littered the Heath were "but a drop in the ocean" in comparison with the millions of trees that were cut down every year to make paper for books that were written by "second rate suburban authors for the purpose of pampering their egos rather than benefitting their readers."

The extremely sensitive writers were incensed; their reaction was to write ever more furiously and copiously, thus requiring even more trees to be felled. The penultimate step was the demand by the environmentalists for Parliament to bring in a law requiring every writer to plant one new tree for every book he sells. The ultimate was reached when Parliament passed such a Bill and the Queen gave it her Royal Assent. Government publications, of course, were excluded from its provisions.

As the Secretary of State predicted, the fire could be seen from all over London. But it didn't have the effect that he intended. From far and near people climbed into their cars and tried to drive towards Hampstead to get a closer look at such a rare and mighty conflagration. And, of course, they added to the already considerable traffic congestion.

Chapter Six

All over London people were having to adjust to the strange circumstances in which they found themselves. Chelsea Pensioners handed out bowls of hot soup to the stranded motorists in Royal Hospital Road, the Superintendent of the Battersea Dogs' Home kept telling his charges how fortunate they were to be born dogs instead of motorists, a cattle truck stuffed with seventy foul smelling pigs was stuck directly outside the door of Knightsbridge's most expensive restaurant for more than three hours and drivers shared food and drink with complete strangers as they had done during the Blitz.

So many babies were born in the back seats of taxis that the cab companies issued special midwife instructions to their drivers over the two way radio. And then there were the romances

And even the conceptions. Men in Maseratis gave the eye to ladies in Lamborghinis, hookers in Hondas smiled at gentlemen in Rolls Royces while Romeos in Renaults threw kisses to spunks in Citroens. Instant affairs between strangers blossomed in the backs of covered vans while a Morris Minor actually rolled over on its side in the King's Road so vigorous was the love-making that went on inside it.

Artists set up easels on the pavement to paint the amazing scene while students from a West End polytech, who had been told to count the cars that passed under Admiralty Arch as part of their project on Modern Urban Living, gave up at 11 a.m. and went to watch a horror movie instead.

The Jehovah's Witnesses made several converts as they

peddled their cheap magazines from car window to car window. Entrepreneurship flourished as gypsies and students took to the roads with sponge and scraper to wash the windscreens of the million plus cars that clogged London's narrow streets.

The gypsies and the students weren't the only ones to be thankful for the chaos; members of the world's most unproductive and unnecessary "profession", the social workers, rubbed their hands in glee at the thought of all the extra work that they could create for themselves by claiming that thousands of people would suffer from "post traffic jam depression" and would therefore require their "counselling services."

To make sure that no one was left outside their interfering net, the social workers of London spent all of Saturday and most of Sunday walking up and down the clogged streets and writing down all the car number plates in their government issue note books. Then, come Monday when they would all be back in their dull, colourless offices in the ghastly, post-war concrete and glass structure that, in former times, might have won an award in a design competition for rabbit hutches, these busybodies, who had a vested job and financial interest in making everyone as psychologically disturbed as possible, would get to work.

First, they would pump all the car number plates into the National Master Computer which would then churn out the names, addresses, occupations, income, etc. of the poor, unsuspecting drivers who, a few days later, would receive a knock on the door from their local social worker.

Like leeches, these mischievous do-gooders always sought out people whom they thought were depressed or miserable. And if the unfortunate victim wasn't depressed from some genuine cause, then a visit from a long-faced, humourless social worker invariably did the trick and inflicted such massive depression that the poor target then required all sorts of visits, chats and therapy to get him right again. All provided, of course, by the burgeoning number of "social workers".

The main query of these ridiculous but expensive creatures

was: "And how are you coping after the terrible traffic jam?"

The reply of the healthy, well-balanced section of society to this apparently innocent but loaded question was : "Very well, thank you. No problems at all," believing that that would be the end of the matter and that the wretched intruder would get out of their living room without further ado. But they failed to take into account the tenacity of the beast that they were up against.

"Yes, well the shock obviously hasn't hit you yet. I'll have to come round again in a few days' time and, if it hasn't struck you by then, we'll give you some therapy to bring it on so that you can confront it and deal with it and get it all out of your system."

Others, whose number plates had been spotted and who were either psychologically hopeless or just plain lonely and wanted someone to chat to (at taxpayer's expense), gave the answer that the intruder wanted: "Well, I haven't been able to sleep so well at nights but I don't know whether it's because of the traffic jam or the heavy metal music that the next door neighbours play until three o'clock every morning."

"It would be the traffic jam—playing on your mind. You'll need therapy. Fill in this thirty-two page form about your past life and we'll feed it into the computer which will churn out a pro-gramme for you. Most of our programmes last three years and involve weekly visits by one of our case officers as well as therapy sessions in the Music Room of the local town hall. It is obvious that you need professional counselling to prevent you going off the tracks and changing your personality as a result of this traumatic experience — you know, becoming an alcoholic, a drug addict, a compulsive gambler or terminating a meaningful rela-tionship with a member of the opposite sex or even of the same sex.

We have special sessions for spouses of 'traffic jamees' on Saturday mornings. Of course, all spouse details will have to be filled out on our special Spouse Form and fed into the Spouse Computer."

On the Monday morning the secretary of the Social Workers And Other Sad Occupations Union addressed his colleagues in the staff cafeteria on the fourth floor of the massive Social Workers' Headquarters building which was the epitome of New Brutalism architecture. "This traffic jam will provide us with more work, which means a bigger budget, more staff and, for those of us who are already a few rungs up the ladder of promotion, the prospect of accelerated advance to the next rung. Almost as good as the aftermath of a massive earthquake." The others nodded their heads at these hopeful words but no one cheered. As social workers they never smiled; the work that they created for themselves was far too depressing for any kind of levity. The only excitment in their dull lives was making dawn raids on unsuspecting parents and snatching their babies from them.

Of more practical use than the career minded social workers were the good men and women of the Salvation Army who set up soup kitchens in local halls and schools to feed the hungry motorists and then, in the evening, provide them with mattresses and blankets for a warm night's sleep.

■
———

Many of the stranded drivers were unable to reach the licensed betting shops to put their money on the horses and greyhounds that were running in different parts of the kingdom. To fill the gap, enterprising shysters started books themselves and went from driver to driver, taking five and ten pound notes and giving in return signed pieces of paper with odds that they had discovered by ringing the betting shops on their car 'phones.

The shops in the High Streets suffered a serious loss of turnover for the day; the only ones that increased their trade were the skateboard shops which, not surprisingly, sold out of all their stock by lunch-time.

There were even queues outside the several knacker's yards on the outskirts of London as people came to realise that a trip on horseback was probably the best way to reach one's destination.

Old nags, for which the dealers had paid a pittance, were now going for hundreds of pounds.

And at Speakers' Corner all the loud mouths complained like mad but no one was able to offer any constructive suggestion as to how to unlock the traffic.

As in the General Strike of 1926, blue-blooded young ladies formed themselves into small teams and passed along the clogged streets of Kensington and Chelsea, distributing glasses of sherry and pieces of fruit cake to the grateful drivers and their passengers.

The least affected were the motor-bike riders. Indeed, the motor-cycle couriers doing their Saturday deliveries were, like the coachmen of old, kings of the road.

The most unlucky motorists of all were those who were trapped within sight of the new Lloyds building. As if being stuck in a traffic jam wasn't bad enough, the fate of having to spend hour after hour looking at London's ugliest and most grotesque architectural horror was more than some of the drivers could bear. Four of them jumped into the freezing Thames and were never heard of again.

Among the more fortunate Londoners on that bleak winter's day were those bibulous and sports minded gentlemen who had gathered in their West End clubs for a lunch time tipple before boarding taxis and specially chartered coaches which would take them to Twickenham. But by midday the club secretaries and organisers had come to the universal conclusion that any such trip was out of the question. Instead, the members ensconced themselves in leather armchairs in the bars of such convivial institutions as the East India, Sports and Public Schools' Club, the Rugby Club and the Wig and Pen Club where they prepared to watch the match on television — fortified, of course, by copious amounts of Scotch and soda to warm their innards and give them the strength to cheer for the British Lions.

It was even better in the evening when they were able to ring their wives or mistresses to say that they were "locked in — just like in a prisoner-of-war camp" and wouldn't be able to make it home through the traffic. "Absolutely impossible, my dear. London's at a complete standstill. Never seen anything like it since the Mafeking celebrations during the Boer War when I sat on my father's shoulders in Trafalgar Square and held on to a bunch of red, white and blue balloons."

"But can't you catch a train? The Underground will be running later on."

"A gentleman doesn't travel on the Underground. No way am I going down there to be exposed to a bunch of hoodlums. At least, not without my swordstick and I've left that at home."

They all returned to their drinks and settled down for a long night of imbibing, reminiscing and singing. It was not long before the hearty strains of *Roll Out The Barrel, Eskimo Nell* and *There'll Always Be An England* were wafting through the warm, smoke filled rooms of Clubland.

■

All roads between Heathrow and Gatwick and Central London were completely blocked; pilots and flight crews were unable to get from their homes and hotels to the airport and airline safety regulations forbade those who had brought the 'planes in from taking them out again. All the airplane bays quickly filled up as everything seemed to be arriving and nothing was leaving.

As more aircraft landed the ground staff frantically wheeled the steps from one 'plane to another. Then at 4 p.m. all the immigration and customs clerks went off duty in accordance with their union rules but only five per cent of the new shift turned up to replace them; the others couldn't get through the traffic. These precious few managed to man a grand total of two desks which caused a logjam of tens of thousands of passengers that stretched all the way to the farthest Arrival Gates. And, of course, there was a record number of transit passengers who couldn't board their onward flights. Old people fainted, babies howled and several passengers had epileptic fits.

The Air Traffic Control Tower was receiving all sorts of unusual queries from their counterparts in Europe.

"When are you going to let us have our 'planes back? We've sent you twenty-two since lunch time and received nothing in return."

"Is Britain such a great place that everyone wants to go there and nobody wants to leave?"

"If you get any more people on that little island of your's it is likely to sink into the sea."

By late afternoon Paris Airport was totally chaotic; all sorts of passengers were missing connecting flights that were meant to come from London and tempers were becoming frayed. Then at ten minutes past four came a polite request from Air Traffic Control, London, that, since Birmingham and Scotland were covered in fog, could all the trans-Atlantic flights to Britain please land at Paris.

"*Mon Dieu!*" exclaimed the senior Air Traffic Controller at Charles de Gaulle Airport. "Why do we have to take all your flights? We have enough of our own."

"Because we have a traffic jam."

"A traffic jam! Where? On the runway or on the motorway?"

"Both."

"Very well, we shall help you. But only because you helped us in the War."

The eighty-six inmates of the House of Confusion, London's most exclusive lunatic asylum situated in leafy Kensington, had been looking forward to Saturday, 17th February, for some time. It was to be the day of one of their rare outings — a trip to the National Portrait Gallery.

They were taken to the Gallery in buses with clouded windows and were accompanied by uniformed and armed minders who were euphemistically described as "social workers".

The lunatics like going to the National Portrait Gallery and seeing paintings of themselves done in better days. Most of them believed that they were King George III and they spent a couple of hours standing in front of his portrait and staring at him in the belief that they were looking in the mirror.

Darwin and Newton inspired similar fascination and when they passed Lord Nelson one of the elderly inmates stared at the missing limbs and observed sagely that the most obvious way of defeating the Russians or any other Navy would be to chop an arm off every Royal Navy officer of the rank of captain and above and pluck out one of their eyes as well.

Another inmate obligingly lifted the portrait of Mrs. Thatcher from the Twentieth Century Room and took it upstairs to the Tudor Room. "She's the one who defeated the Argentine Armada," one of them explained. "You know, when Sir Francis Drake sank the General Belgrano." It was all very confusing.

No one noticed the change of pictures. The minders were too busy sharpening their knives and other weapons while all the ancient, uniformed pensioners who were meant to be guarding the paintings had been curled up asleep in their chairs since the 1930s; they hadn't even been disturbed by the Blitz. In their sleep they had heard the drone of the Spitfires and Dorniers but thought it was just the unusually loud snoring of their colleagues.

One of the lunatics was so affected by Augustus John's drawing of Lawrence of Arabia that he lifted a white dust sheet off a pile of paintings in the corner, draped it over his head and ran round the gallery asking all the men of military age if they would like to join the Arab Legion.

At 3 p.m. the vile looking minders started to round them all up with horse whips for the journey back to Kensington. But this time the buses with the clouded windows couldn't get through the traffic; so they had to walk all the way back to the asylum in a long, winding column.

When they saw all the stationary traffic clogging the streets the lunatics were utterly amazed. Nothing as crazy as that had ever been seen in the House of Confusion. As one of them said with stunning clarity: "Cars are made for moving from one point to another. They have no other purpose. Yet these strange people sit in cars that don't move; it really is confusing."

"Why do they keep sitting in their cars instead of walking? Like us! At least we'll soon be back at the House of Confusion whereas these silly people will still be here."

"Perhaps we should build another fence around our institution. In case they try to break in. We wouldn't want to be like them, would we?"

"No way. In half an hour we'll all be sitting down to a nice hot meal and they'll still be sitting here in the cold looking at the car in front of them."

"I think I've got the answer!" exclaimed Lawrence of Arabia.

"What?" cried all the George the Thirds.

"They should destroy all their cars."

"But then how would the silly fools get around?"

"On camels."

∎

And the police? Well, they stood around waving their arms and blowing their whistles and trying to look as if they were doing something but, as Colonel Byng-Moresby observed, they were "about as much use as if they were on a comedy show."

The emergency services were grounded; no matter how loudly they screamed their sirens they couldn't move an inch. A furniture store burnt down in Chelsea while a tyre factory in Clapham sent up a huge cloud of black smoke that could be seen and smelt all over Central London. And, on top of everything else, the evil vermin and scum in the I.R.A. had chosen this particular afternoon to blow up the maternity wing of a London hospital on the perverse grounds that the doctor in charge had once served in a Belfast hospital where he had saved the life of a young soldier who had been shot by terrorists.

This massacre of the babies was roundly condemned by all sides with the exception of one twisted, gin-sodden politician in Dublin who claimed on television that it was all the fault of the British Government for not providing armour plated maternity hospitals.

As night fell the theatres of Shaftesbury Avenue found that they were less than half full. Most of the patrons, who had bought tickets during the week, were unable to get anywhere near the West End. Not surprisingly one of the stranded drivers, who had been sitting outside the same theatre looking at the same billing of an Oscar Wilde play since mid-morning, suggested to the manager that he might like to let in some of the cold, bored motorists gratuitously to fill the many empty seats. The manager looked horrified. "Good God, no. We could never do that," he said.

"Why not?"

"Because it might create a precedent."

Some of the worst mix-ups occurred at the churches where weddings were thrown into complete confusion. In some places the bridegroom had turned up but not the bride; elsewhere it was the other way round. Some churches had guests but no wedding party and in one Romanesque pile everyone was there except the greedy Irish priest who, a couple of hours earlier, had driven to the betting shop in his brand new BMW and was now well and truly stranded in the traffic.

In another church everyone had arrived for the five o'clock wedding except the bridal party who had to travel all the way from Hertfordshire. However, the ceremony went ahead without them.

A couple of blocks from the church Merv from Manchester, in a left-hand drive Volkswagen Kombi, had been sitting in a stationary line of traffic since 10.30 a.m. In order to while away the time he had wound down his window and started talking to the driver of the Singer Gazelle beside him. Topsy from Tottenham, being in a right-hand vehicle as well as in the nearside lane, found herself only a few inches away from her talkative neighbour.

Between half past ten and twelve he told her all about his

77

past life, between twelve and one she poured out the details of her life, between one and two they planned the future together and from two to four they were locked in tight embrace in the back of the van getting to know each other more intimately. And, shortly after four, they climbed out of the van and went in search of someone with the legal power to marry them.

When they turned up at the church which contained minister, guests, choir and hymn sheets but no bride and groom the vicar was only too happy to substitute them for the unfortunately absent participants and everything went ahead as planned — except that the vicar changed "Norton and Pamela" to "Merv and Topsy."

The worst chaos occurred at the church of Saint Thomas and the Doubters where everyone turned up for both the half past twelve funeral and the two o'clock wedding.

The late Mr. Jack Rotgut had sat in the House of Commons as a Labour Party Member. On the extreme Left of that deeply fragmented party. He died from a massive heart attack (captured live by the B.B.C.) as he was addressing the House on the Second Schedule of the Compulsory Registration of Seagulls in Coastal Areas Bill.

Several of his colleagues turned up at the church which was only a few blocks from Westminster. They heard the vicar praise the deceased for all the strikes and other trouble that he had caused while he was alive; this was followed by a fiery denunciation of the Conservative Government which was blamed for every known evil in Britain, Europe and the wider world. "They should give more money to the poor!" thundered the vicar who, as usual, forgot to mention that his own church was sitting on an investment fund of more than a billion pounds, none of which ever seemed to go to the poor.

The problem for Rotgut, M.P. was that he had been delivered to the church in his pine box the previous night and now the hearse was unable to get through the traffic to collect him for the onward journey to the crematorium.

After the service the comrades lingered on — talking about

this and that. When to call the next strike, how to take over this constituency and that constituency, how to con the public into voting for them, how to suck even more money out of the workers in the form of union fees so that the union bosses could pay off their flash holiday homes in Spain.

"Looks like we'll have to leave the body in the church until the traffic clears," said Pete Gabble, M.P., the leader of the Extreme Left faction. "Maybe over night. That won't be a problem, will it, Vicar?"

"Well........"

"Problem?"

"Yes. I've got a wedding here in half an hour. Gosh, here come the first of the guests. Wonder how they got through the traffic. They probably live nearby since the bridegroom's family is prominent in the political world."

"Who?"

"Sir Rover Getover."

"Sir Rover Getover! You mean that bastard who owns all those thousands of acres up in Yorkshire?"

"Yes. I think it's the same one," said the vicar sheepishly.

"Why do you let types like that get married in your church?"

"Well....the church funds were right down and he did slip me a couple of thousand. Look, you know that I'm on your side and against capitalism; if I had my way, everyone with more than twenty thousand pounds worth of assets would be lined up against a wall and shot at dawn. But my primary task is to obtain money for my church and — for what it's worth — I don't ever get a donation from the unions. So I just have to skin these wealthy people and even let their sons and daughters get married in the church until such time as I can draw sufficient funds from elsewhere."

"Hello Vicar!" roared Sir Rover as he strode up the church steps with his grandly dressed wife for what they both hoped would be one of the major society weddings of the year. Sir Rover was ex-Guards, ex-City and would soon be ex-House of Com-

79

mons; he was retiring as a Member of the Commons in the hope of being elevated to "another place".

"Why aren't the church bells ringing?" asked Sir Rover. "It has just been announced on the radio that Her Majesty's Secretary of State for Transport has ordered that the church bells be rung all over London to warn people not to drive their cars. It would only add to the congestion and it's bad enough as it is. Thank God the reception is just round the corner. All the guests can walk. Yes, let's ring the bells; besides, this is a happy occasion. The wedding of my only son. Lady Getover and I hope to be presented with a grandson and heir in nine months' time. That's why we want to hear the joyous peal of the church bells."

"Not so fast, Getover," said Pete Gabble. "We've got a dead man in there. One of our comrades. Surely you wouldn't be so insensitive as to ring out the bells of joy on the occasion of the death of a fellow Member of Parliament?"

"Nonsense!" cried Sir Rover. "I've always said that the only good Labour M.P. is a dead one. I've even said that in the House. Look it up in Hansard if you don't believe me."

He took the vicar aside. "Listen, Vicar. That cheque. Have you banked it yet?"

"Yes."

"When?"

"Yesterday afternoon."

"Then it won't yet be cleared and I can still put a Stop on it. And if the bells aren't ringing in five minutes that's exactly what I'll do." The vicar went white. "Look, there are the bell-ringers," continued Sir Rover. "Get to it, boys! As much noise as you can make. It's been ordered by the Secretary of State for Transport. You'll be performing a service for the nation."

Four minutes later the heavy bells of Saint Thomas and the Doubters were being pulled for all they were worth. It was Round One to the Tories.

"That's better," said Sir Rover as he walked from the porch into the nave of the church. "What's that?" he exclaimed when he saw the big oblong box at the front of the aisle. It was covered with a red flag in the top corner of which was a black hammer and sickle.

"That's the late Mister Rotgut," replied the vicar. "The hearse can't get through the traffic to collect him and we've got nowhere else to put him. Can't leave him out on the street."

"Why not?"

"Someone might attack the box. After all, he wasn't very popular, was he?"

Sir Rover looked up towards the Gothic spire — as if for guidance. Then he turned to the vicar and said, "The reason why the hearse can't come here to collect the body is because of the traffic jam. The reason for the traffic jam is the blocking of the bridges by the left wing councillors who are connected with the same faction in the Labour Party as the late Mister Rotgut. Therefore, Rotgut and his friends here are the architects of their own misfortune. They caused the problem; it's over to them to solve it — by getting rid of the box and the filthy piece of material that's draped over it. Thirty million innocent people were murdered in the Soviet Union by the Party of the hammer and sickle and yet these creeps have the nerve to display it in our own free and happy country. Get a hurry on!"

"But....." The vicar was almost in tears. "Don't you have any Christian charity in you, sir? Can't you make an exception for one of your fellow human beings? One of your fellow Members of Parliament?"

"Stalin didn't make any exceptions when he went round murdering his millions, did he? Worse bugger than Hitler. And another thing."

"Yes?"

"I used to serve in India. During the Raj. When India was governed properly. Not like now when they have a new government every week. And one thing I learned out there is that the Hindus believe in reincarnation and spirits. And I'm not prepared to say that they're wrong. When people get married in India everything has to be auspiciously arranged. *No bad spirits.* If there's one lying around — like a lazy pi dog — then it has to be chased away. And if they can't get rid of the bad spirit, then they put the wedding off until a more promising day. And I don't want any bad spirits or omens around here to curse the union of my only son with his beautiful, blue blooded wife. And I couldn't think of a more evil spirit than that of Rotgut. I don't want him anywhere near this church while the wedding is taking place. Hell, we'd never get that grandson in nine months with Rotgut at the wedding."

"Well where are we going to put him?"

"In the red 'phone box down the road. He likes the colour red, doesn't he? He'd fit in the telephone box. Upright, of course. I'll even loan him my 'phone card. He might like to make a long distance call."

"Where on earth to?"

"To Hell, of course. To book his place!"

"But....."

"Come on! Six strong men please. Military men if possible. We'll march with precision."

Six of his guests volunteered their services and the body of the late Jack Rotgut was duly placed in the telephone box — standing upright and with Sir Rover's green 'phone card resting in the machine lest the deceased might like to make the suggested call. It was Round Two to the Tories.

Pete Gabble and his comrades stood guard at the 'phone box while the rest of the funeral congregation adjourned to the nearest pub to discuss the evil, heartless capitalist class as personified by Sir Rover Getover.

When they returned, the Tory pall-bearers of the Labour Member of Parliament all bent down and washed their hands under the tap outside the church door. "Such a distasteful task. Best to wash our hands," said one of them.

"Such a distasteful fellow!" replied the others.

By now all the guests were in their places awaiting the

arrival of the bride and her father. The vicar was standing in his robes at the foot of the altar with the prayer book in his hand when........suddenly, he toppled over. After all the events of the last half hour the poor man had fainted. He hit his head on the stone floor and was concussed. It happened just as the choir began singing Mendelssohn's beautiful hymn to herald the arrival of the bride and her father who had walked to the church from their nearby house.

Sir Rover was out of his pew in a flash. He ran straight to the vicar and sat him up on the floor. "I feel dizzy," the cleric kept saying.

"Here, have a little of this," said Sir Rover who handed him what appeared to be a larger than usual Alternate Service Book.

"But I've already got my prayer book," mumbled the vicar who was more confused than ever.

"And what's inside it?"

"Pages of prayers and psalms. Why, what's inside your's?"

"Whisky. Neat. Just what you need. See the cork in the top. Pull it off and take a couple of swigs. We'll have you right in no time."

"Well I never!" exclaimed the vicar as he drank the twenty-five year old Scotch and began to feel better. "I've never seen a whisky flask in the shape of a prayer book before."

"All my friends in Parliament have got them. We'd never be able to survive all those boring memorial services at Saint Margaret's without them. Most precious possession an M.P. can have. Quick, stand up! The bride's on her way."

The bump on the head must have affected the vicar's brain; towards the end of the ceremony he mounted the steps of the pulpit to announce how fortunate the bride was to be marrying into such a kind, Christian family as the Getovers. "There is no more generous benefactor of our church than the saintly Sir Rover. In his everyday life as well as in his utterances in the House he has marked himself out as a firm soldier of Christ who is always on the side of the poor and the unfortunate." Sir Rover gave a smug smile from his position in the front pew on the bridegroom's side of the church.

"We hear a lot of words from those on the Left," continued the vicar, "but that is all they are — words! It is left to men like Sir Rover to provide the deeds. As I said at the earlier service, anyone with less than twenty thousand pounds in the bank should be put up against a wall and shot at dawn." Boom! The vicar had a massive brain haemorrhage and fell down dead in full view of all the guests. Those on the bride's side got the better view.

"Jolly considerate of him to snuff it in the church," chortled Sir Rover to his wife.

"Why?"

"We can pop him in that tomb over there. The one between Anne Boleyn's uncle and Lord Thumpington's favourite mistress. The thing's been empty for years. The vicar will be a perfect fit. After all those nice things he said about me I'm happy to pay for the top to be sealed and a brass plaque with his name on it. And something like 'He fell in the course of his duty'."

The guests all filed outside the church. They complimented the bride on her dress and politely confined the conversation to the weather, the traffic jam and Sir Rover's black silk top hat. This was a Society Wedding and dead vicars fell outside the bounds of polite conversation.

After the photographs were taken the guests all made off down the street in the direction of the reception which was, in fact, only two blocks away.

The men of Gabble's group had long become tired of playing sentries at the telephone booth so they joined the others in the pub.

"Old Jack always liked his beer. His favourite was Newcastle Brown," remembered one of them.

"And underneath his dour public image he always liked a joke too. As long as it was a working class joke."

"Hey, that gives me an idea."

"What?"

"Why don't we buy a pint of Geordie juice and take it out to him?"

"Good idea!" roared the others.

The pint was duly purchased and carried outside to the telephone box. They were feeling quite merry and had no qualms at removing the red flag and opening the coffin. Rotgut stared at them with his mouth open.

"Here you are, Jack. We've brought you a pint of Geordie juice. Your favourite."

They rested his elbow on the inside screw of one of the handles and tried to put the glass in Rotgut's hand. But it kept slipping.

One of them ran off to the shop and bought some super glue. They cut the tube open and squeezed it on to the outside of the glass as well as the palm of the dead man's hand. For the next few minutes they held the glass steady until the glue set. When they eventually let go, the glass remained stuck to Rotgut's hand without spilling.

"Shall we give him a swig?" one of them asked.

"No point in rushing the dead. If he really wants a sip he'll raise the glass to his mouth and take one." With that they all returned to the pub to buy another round.

The wedding guests stared in amazement as they walked past the telephone box on their way to the reception.

"Who's he?" asked one of them.

"We think he's something to do with the councillors who blocked the bridges," replied one of the stranded motorists. "That's why we're leaving him there. Shame they're not all in boxes. And I don't mean telephone boxes."

When Sir Rover and his crowd walked past the 'phone booth his sister-in-law pointed to the corpse's open mouth.

"That's because he was a Labour M.P.," laughed Sir Rover. "Always got their mouths open. Usually with a whole lot of rubbish coming out in the form of words."

"You mean that poor man was a Member of Parliament and

now he's finished up in a 'phone box?" exclaimed the horrified lady.

"That's the Labour Party for you. No class!" said Sir Rover with a smug look on his face. Third and Final Round to the Tories.

Chapter Seven

After he left Chequers Myles rode through the gentle fields of Buckinghamshire to the Mad Clown public house where the chapter had decided to take their afternoon refreshments. He drew to a stop on the cobble stones outside the public bar and parked his bike under the hand-painted sign and portrait of a mad clown that hung from a high gable. He could see the others' well-kept machines parked on the roadway and in the deserted beer garden. He tied his helmet to the handle bars and ran inside out of the cold. A topless waitress brushed past him and took his order.

"Hey, Myles, what did Maggie give you? A knighthood or a tax exemption?"

"Well, nothing actually but she was jolly grateful."

"Do you think she'll come for another ride with us? Maybe at Easter? Of course, we're all going to vote for her next time. After all, she's now a bikie just like us. We thought she'd fall off."

"No way. She was as steady as a rock. I knew she would be. That's why I agreed to take her."

"Hey, babe," yelled Spider, the oldest member of the chapter, "get us another round of Carling Black Label. One of us has just come from Chequers; the Prime Minister has been riding with us." The buxom lass took some of their empty glasses, leaned her head back, rested a couple of them on her breasts and walked carefully up to the bar.

In the alcove over by the corner Jackal was getting along very nicely with Barmaid Betty. "What time do you finish here to-night?" he whispered in her ear.

"I'm on the early shift. Finish at seven."

"Then I'll wait around and we can go to some local barn for a romp in the hay."

"No, my boyfriend's coming to collect me. Then we're going to London."

"Ha! Boyfriends! Boyfriends have never worried the Angels. Maybe we could meet up in London?"

"We're going to an acid house party in the East End. It's all very hush hush. Has to be. You know what the cops are like. They hate to see young people having a good time so they come round and smash up all the acid house parties."

"I hate acid heads," said Jackal. "We Angels regard them as boring little children. I wouldn't be seen dead at an acid house party. But I won't tell the police. We hate them even more than acid heads."

"It's being held in an old warehouse. The only one left standing on some deserted industrial estate that suffered bomb damage in the Blitz and no one has ever built on it. Until now. You see, they're going to put up a housing estate and shopping centre there and so the owner of this last warehouse is throwing a big party and at the end we're all going to smash the building down. Saves him having to pay the costs of demolition."

"Well in that case the Angels will be there. What's the address?"

"Can't give you that," she whispered. "Top secret. But if you meet up with the rest of us at midnight outside Stratford Tube Station you'll get there. None of us knows exactly where it is but there'll be a couple of marshals in dark glasses and they'll be at the station at midnight and will lead us there. Sorry, but I must start collecting the glasses. Don't want to get the sack." Jackal loosened his grip on her and she bounced up and began clearing the nearby tables.

"Well," said Jackal when he rejoined the others, "our little trip has been worthwhile. I've found out about a top secret party in the East End to-night. Although we'll have to put up with acid heads for a few hours it'll all be worthwhile because at the end of the show we're gonna knock the warehouse down. So, bring your sledgehammers, boys. Any shirkers?"

"Yes, one. Count me out," said Myles. "I really must work on that bloody brief to-night. I'm due to stand up in court on Monday morning and I haven't even looked at it — let alone understood it."

"Listen, mate, there won't be any court on Monday. No one'll be able to get through the traffic."

"Well the judge will be there," said Myles. "They mostly live at the Inns of Court and, if necessary, they could walk to the Bailey. Or, at least, some of the younger ones could."

"But what about the jury? They'll have to come from all over London. If they don't turn up, you can't proceed with the case."

"Unfortunately we can."

"How?"

"The officers of the court will pray the tails."

"What's that mean? They all go and kneel at Saint Paul's?"

"No. It's an ancient custom whereby, if there are not enough jurors, the court officials go out on the street and nab the first passers-by they see and drag them in to sit on the jury. And by law you can't refuse. It reflects the principle that jury service is a duty of the citizen rather than a privilege."

"Well, that's solved. Me and my friends, we'll all go and hang round outside the door of the court so that when the official comes out we'll be the first twelve people he sees and he'll drag us in to sit on the jury. I mean, we'd be acceptable because we don't know the criminal, do we? We'll even wear our respectable clothes.

We'll listen to what the court has to say, then we'll retire for ten minutes to have a smoke in the jury room and then we'll return and say 'Not Guilty!' The guy'll get off, you'll get your fee and it'll be one less for the poor old British taxpayer to support in prison. Everyone will be happy. We'll be twelve men good and true."

"If only it were as simple as that!" thought Myles.

■
———————

Shortly after Myles had left the house to ride with the Angels Annabelle arrived at Aston Square. Fiona met her on the doorstep and the two of them set off for Portobello Road. They drove as far as the entrance to the Square where they sat for twenty minutes waiting to get into the line of traffic that had been at a complete standstill for nearly two hours.

"We'll just have to walk," said Fiona as she reversed Myles' car back along the Square to the parking place outside Number Eighteen.

As she was locking the car she could hear the 'phone ringing inside the house. Dashing up the steps, she unlocked the front door and grabbed the receiver.

The caller was Derek Wiggle, her agent, who provided her with a lot of excellent work for television commercials. He was a member of the firm of Gribble, Nibble and Wiggle which had sprung to prominence in the early Eighties and had since fed off the seemingly endless advertising budgets of businesses large and small that had prospered in the new era of lower taxes and a market led economy.

Derek Wiggle was forty-nine, divorced, obese and forever on the lookout for an opportunity — usually the chance to bed the particular model for whom he was currently finding work. But not Fiona. She was far too sought after in her profession to have to sink to such inducements in order to obtain assignments. Besides, she regarded the slick, greasy haired, aspiring Romeo with a combination of wariness and revulsion. But he had given her some valuable work which — even after his commission — had been responsible for putting several thousand pounds into her bank account.

The latest opportunity that the wandering eye of Derek Wiggle had spotted was the traffic jam. Or, more correctly, the combination of the traffic jam and the recent request from the world's largest manufacturer of motor-bike helmets to find an "original" ad to kick start their new line of headgear which was to be marketed world wide under the brand name of "Going Places."

"Ah, Fiona," came the deep husky voice from the other end of the line. "Thank God I caught you at home. All this traffic has given us a God sent opportunity to make a truly unique commercial for the new line of crash helmets. Can you get to Buckingham Palace as soon as possible?"

"Buckingham Palace! What shall I wear? My debutante's dress?"

"No, black leather pants and leather jacket. The tighter the better. I want you to ride a motor-bike down the middle of the Mall. Between the lines of stationary cars. The photographer will be standing on the top of Admiralty Arch with a telephoto lens and you'll ride towards him. It'll look great; you'll be the only one getting anywhere. Everything else will be static. The best way of marketing *Going Places* helmets that I can think of."

"What time and how much? I'm just on my way to Portobello Road with my friend."

"Ah, the best laid plans can be torn asunder. I'll send the bike to your house with a driver. He should be there in half an hour. That'll give you time to change. The photographer is already on his way to Admiralty Arch. The fee will be a thousand pounds."

Fiona put down the receiver and informed Annabelle of the change of plans. "So sorry, Belle, but I can't turn down a thousand pounds."

"Oh, all right. I'll go to Portobello on my own and see what I can find."

It took Fiona forty minutes to apply her make-up and change into the leather clothes that were left over from a previous motor-bike commercial. When she opened the front door she heard the driver revving his machine as he turned into the square from the traffic clogged thoroughfare outside. The shy young man introduced himself and Fiona climbed on the back of the bike. They weaved their way through the traffic until they came to the great open space in front of the Queen's official residence.

The ubiquitous Derek Wiggle was already there, having walked from his office in Hanover Square. He was huffing and puffing from the physical effort of his short hike and Fiona sincerely believed that he would have a heart attack and drop dead right where they were standing.

The agent was holding a wig of long blond hair and a luminous green crash helmet with the words "Going Places" painted across its top in bold, black lettering.

"Put these on!" he panted. "We want to have at least three feet of hair blowing in the breeze underneath the helmet." Fiona did what she was told; it wasn't much to bear for a thousand pounds.

She climbed on the bike behind the Queen Victoria Memorial and Wiggle switched on his two way radio to tell the photographer at the other end of the Mall that they were ready.

Fiona started the machine and drove it out from the Memorial at a careful but steady pace. She wended her way between the stationary cars and headed towards the single empty lane that ran down the middle of the grandest avenue in the world as far as Admiralty Arch. The photographer captured it all — including her face when she looked up and smiled as she approached the Arch. *Going Places* helmets had certainly got off to a wonderful start.

Afterwards they all met in a small pub in Buckingham Palace Road— the photographer, the shy young driver, the still breathless Derek Wiggle and Fiona. The sleek haired agent explained how the film just shot would constitute only the second part of the ad. "And what will you use for the first half?" asked Fiona who was hoping for possibly a further assignment worth another thousand pounds.

"All the Queen's horses and all the Queen's men parading down the same stretch of road on their way to the Trooping of the

Colour. That bit's being included for the American market. They love all our pageantry and royalty."

As they were leaving, Derek Wiggle whispered to Fiona that he had two tickets for Covent Garden that evening and would she like to go with him and have "a little something" afterwards.

"No thanks, Derek. I don't like to mix business with pleasure. Creates too many problems. Good God, look at that! This traffic jam really is turning up some amazing sights."

They stood in the doorway of the pub and watched a uniformed butler pushing his white haired, crippled milord along the footpath in a wheelchair.

"Must be on his way to the doctor or the hospital," said a sympathetic Fiona.

"Or perhaps an afternoon tryst with his young mistress," replied Gribble with a twinge of envy.

Chapter Eight

The American lawyers and judges who were attending the law conference were scattered and lost throughout the area of Greater London, their ordeal being all the worse by virtue of the fact that most of them couldn't understand the London A to Z.

"Why the hell aren't the streets numbered like they are in New York?" screamed one distraught attorney from Manhattan who was looking for Oxford University in Oxford Street. "I'm just about out of my mind. Yesterday my boy wanted to go to the circus so I took him to Piccadilly Circus but there was no circus. Just a whole lot of damned traffic. Then he wanted to go to the zoo so we went to Elephant and Castle. Same problem — no elephants and no castle. So we decided to go boating instead. I took him to Bayswater but there was neither a bay nor water. If you ask me this whole damned city is just one huge fraud on the tourist. There's no hay in the Haymarket, White City isn't even a city, Mister Heath doesn't live on Hampstead Heath and at Gray's Inn they all wear black instead of gray. Hell man, if you come to New York and you want to find 42nd Street it's between 41st and 43rd Streets. Even a dumb limey cop would be able to find it."

"Yes, sir, but our city is a little older than your's," replied the polite young constable on the beat to whom this diatribe had been directed. "And I believe that our streets are a little bit safer. One is less likely to be mugged on the London Underground than in the New York subways."

"You're sure right there, officer. At least for to-day. No one will be getting mugged on your Tube to-day. The thing aint even runnin'."

The confused attorney wasn't the only one of his country's legal fraternity who was trapped and lost in the traffic. Judge Mohawk Terracotta and his wife, Firma, had driven out to Heathrow to meet Judge Hiram Puncher and District Attorney Lurlene Daisy Puncher. The Punchers were a deadly husband and wife team; she prosecuted them and he sentenced them. They were doubly pro-death—in favour of both abortion and the death penalty.

The reason for the Punchers' late arrival in London was that the good judge had decided to stay behind in Florida to oversee the electrocution of six young men and a woman whom he had sentenced to death earlier in the year. When Puncher walked through the Arrivals Gate at Heathrow he had come direct from the killing fields and had barely had time to wash the blood of the condemned souls from his hands.

"Hello, Hiram. How did it go?" asked Mohawk.

"Wonderful. A full house. Many judges, lawyers, cops, prison officers and, of course, the usual crowd of cheering people outside the prison walls. It was great fun.

They even televised the last meal. Nationwide. Drew a bigger viewing audience than the Inauguration of the President. Of course, the guards had put bits of broken glass and dogshit into the apple tart. Gave everyone a great laugh.

Some of the local radio stations urged everyone to turn off their electrical appliances — frigidaires and all that — so as to give the bastards the largest shot of electricity possible. The people responded admirably. Made them feel they were part of the electrifying process. But I was right there and saw all the flames and smoke shoot out of their heads. Just like on Fireworks Night. I've always said that the sight of a man on the electric chair is what makes the job so rewarding. It's the ultimate feeling of power."

"Do you mean 'power' as in strength and importance or 'power' as in electricity?" was the punnish comment of Judge Terracotta. They all roared with laughter. "Thank God we still do it with the Chair. Not like in Texas where they've switched to lethal injections; that's what I call the coward's way out. Injections are so boring; no fun at all. My God, I hope we never give up the Chair in Florida."

"If we did," said Puncher, "do you know what I'd like it to be replaced with?"

"No."

"Crucifixion. It would prolong the pain."

"What a brilliant idea! I've never thought of that one."

"Yes, but I'd make the bastards carry their own cross up a hill first. A real steep one that's hard to climb — not like that little hill in Jerusalem. Far too small. And then I'd nail the rotters to the cross with those big lead-headed four inch nails — the ones you use on the roof. And think of the television potential!"

"Fantastic! Let's put it to the State Governor when we get back home. It should be enough to get him re-elected."

"Tell me, Mohawk, what's this hotel like where we're all staying?"

"It's brand new — believe it or not. Most of their hotels are left over from the Roman era but this one was completed only a few months ago. Built to a traditional design, of course. Very central. In fact, only a couple of hundred yards from Waterloo Station."

"Great! I've always wanted to see the spot where Napoleon was defeated. How far away is it?"

"We were two hours in the traffic coming out here. Hopefully the return journey will be quicker." But it wasn't.

They got trapped in a line of vehicles on the M4 that was moving at the pace of the proverbial snail. All four of them nagged the driver so much that he decided to exit at the next off ramp and head in a southerly direction for the river. He knew of the chaos that was taking place on the bridges further downstream and reasoned that, since their hotel was on the South Bank, it would be better to get across the Thames as soon as possible. The driver was a follower of the round ball and knew nothing about rugby; in fact, he didn't even know that there was a match being played at Twickenham. Which was why he drove through Hounslow and then straight into the Great Twickenham Traffic Jam. Where they stayed for the rest of the afternoon. And all night.

The American judges and their wives were appalled and made all sorts of helpful suggestions to the driver like "Why don't you pull down all these old houses and replace them with free-ways?" and "Can't the Queen send a couple of her horses for us? After all, we are here at the invitation of Her Majesty's judges."

At five o'clock some sixty thousand people began to emerge from Twickenham — all cheering, singing and throwing their brightly coloured scarves into the air.

"Get down! Get down! We're about to be attacked by football hooligans," screamed a terrified Judge Puncher. He didn't mind killing others but he had no wish to be killed himself.

"They won't attack you," laughed the driver. "They're rugby supporters — not soccer hooligans. All their fighting is done on the pitch — in front of everyone. It's the other way round in football; they wait until after the game to use their knives and fists. But these people you see now, they're all gentlemen. From some of our best schools."

"Well they don't look much like gentlemen to me," quivered Puncher. "More like delinquents."

"I know that it must be hard for you gentlemen from the New World to understand all the subtleties of English society but I'll try to explain. See those slash marks on the upholstery of the seat you're sitting on."

"Yes, I was wondering about those," said Terracotta.

"Well, they were done this morning by a group of football supporters whom I drove to their game. But rugby followers wouldn't do that. All they would do is smash an empty whisky bottle on the floor but they'd be careful not to damage the seats. You see, that's the difference. The ones you're seeing now are gentlemen. The ones who always lead Britain in battle. If you take a closer look you'll see that they're all wearing their regimental ties."

The judges and their wives were even more amazed when

they saw a couple of Highland pipers come marching round the corner playing *Scotland The Brave*.

"Now what sort of country have you got over here? There are no police or soldiers to control the traffic; they're all too busy dressing up and blowing bagpipes!"

The music stopped and the two pipers, with typical Caledonian canniness, walked along the cars with their hands out for whatever gratuity the motorists were prepared to offer.

"Good God, look at that!" exclaimed Puncher. "They're not even soldiers. Just buskers dressed up as soldiers."

"Trust the jocks to make something out of it!" laughed the driver.

Their attention was distracted by some yelling on the footpath. They looked across and saw a black uniformed traffic warden having a loud argument with a young driver of a Porsche who was complaining about a parking infringement notice that had just been tucked under his left windscreen wiper.

"You overstayed on the metre. It's a thirty pound fine," said the uniformed man whose lowly origins, in an earlier age, would have put him in domestic service doing something useful like polishing the silver or waiting on his master at table instead of prowling the streets of modern Britain like a plague.

"Yes, but we can't get out. Can't you see the traffic jam? Or perhaps, Mister Hitler, you're too preoccupied with throwing your weight around to notice. I came back an hour ago and couldn't get out so I went over to the common with my missus for a romp. I didn't have any more money on me to feed the metre and anyway, since it wasn't my fault that I overstayed, I didn't reckon that I could be given a ticket."

"Well you reckoned wrongly, Mister Smart Alec. The law is the law and it is my job to enforce it on cars that have overstayed on metres. *Regardless of the circumstances*," retorted the warden whose face was fast turning green with envy as he looked at the beautiful, shining vehicle and compared it to his own rusted, second-hand Lada that was broken down on the road outside his mean council flat in the wilds of Haringey. He always enjoyed issuing tickets to the drivers of expensive cars. It was the only way he could get his own back on a society in which he had never risen from the lowest rung. While others had well-paid jobs, attractive wives and nice, big houses he had never been able to rise above being a parking warden — trudging through the cold and rainy streets, being abused and despised by the rest of the population, never smiling, never being asked to nice parties and receiving only a pittance of an income that was not unconnected with the fact that his job was one of the lowest and most unskilled in the land. The only redeeming feature of his miserable existence was being able to put infringement notices on the cars of his betters and take sadistic delight in their annoyance. Like now.

"Now look here," screamed the irate driver, "if you don't take that filthy piece of paper off my windscreen right this minute I'll make you wish that you'd chosen a more worthwhile job than terrorising motorists."

The warden just stood there with a smug look on his thin, mean looking face. Whack! The driver struck him a powerful punch in the left eye. Then the right one. A group of flask swilling rugby supporters were walking past and witnessed the whole thing.

"You champion!" one of them cried to the heroic driver. "If you need any witnesses we'll all come to court and say that he struck you first. Here, take a swig. Black label. Neat. Bought it duty free on my way back from Amsterdam last week-end."

"Thanks. Just what I need."

By now the downed parking warden was lying on the road in considerable pain and squealing like a pig. A few of the pedestrians gave him a kick as they walked past.

"Is he dead?" asked one.

"No."

"Pity. Better luck next time."

The Americans in the cab could hardly believe their eyes. Mohawk Terracotta turned to the driver and said, "If that happened in Florida that cop would have drawn his gun and fired away non-stop. All those people who abused him would now be dead bodies strewn across the sidewalk."

"That's why we don't give guns to our men in uniform," replied the driver.

"What do you mean?"

"Well, you saw the way that little creep conducted himself, didn't you? He was officious and arrogant enough as it was. Give him a gun and he'd be a real Hitler instead of a make-believe one."

"They sure don't seem to have much authority over here, do they?" put in Puncher.

"No. What they need is a posse of gun totin' Miami cops. They'd soon get the traffic moving."

The two judges then turned their attention to the more functional problem of getting back to their hotel in time to change for the judges' dinner that their British counterparts were putting on for them in the ancient and ornate dining hall at the Inns of Court. Dinner was at seven and it was already half past five.

"How much longer are we going to be in this goddammed traffic jam?" asked Mohawk Terracotta.

"Dunno," said the driver as he pulled out a packet of Rothmans and lit another cigarette.

■

Meanwhile at the Inns of Court their judicial hosts were just putting the lid on their learned activities for the day in order to ready themselves for dinner. They lived, worked and dined within the walls of the Inns of Court where many of them had luxurious grace and favour apartments that were a perk of the job. So neat and compact were their lives that they rarely ever had to leave the cloistered confines of the Inns to mix with the ordinary folk whom they were forever judging.

By six o'clock these frail old men were busy dressing for

dinner in their frock coats, striped trousers, stiff collars and black gowns. To a man they were completely ignorant of the traffic chaos that was being borne by the rest of London. All day they had been safely ensconced in their chambers, flats and libraries reading their cases and looking up the most obscure points of law in the hundred year old books that lined the dusty shelves. Football was no part of their world and nor were traffic jams.

It was a little after twenty to seven when the last of them shuffled across the stone courtyard to their Pension Room where they were to receive their American counterparts before leading them into the Great Hall for dinner. The only problem was that there were no American judges anywhere within a cuckoo's call of the Inns or indeed a long way beyond. They were scattered all over London in their stationary taxis staring at the rear ends of the vehicles in front of them.

"I must say it's jolly rude of them not to turn up on time," said the Treasurer, Lord Justice Poppyseed as he absent-mindedly flicked his cigarette ash into the silver snuff box.

"Perhaps we told them the wrong night. After all, it's extremely unlikely that they'd *all* make the same mistake. I must say that it does put a bit of a dent in my life-long belief in the infallibility of the judiciary."

"Yes, but it's *American* judges who have made this mistake, Sir Giles. *Not* English judges. I mean, we're all here, aren't we? The mistake hasn't been made on our side of the Atlantic."

"Oh dear!" moaned Sir Peregrine Periwinkle who had recently celebrated his hundredth birthday. "I knew that it was a mistake to invite all these colonials to dinner. It seems only yesterday that we were fighting them in the War of Independence."

"And let's not forget that some of them are murderers," said one of the others who, at seventy, was the youngest in the Room.

"Judicial murderers," corrected the Treasurer.

"Yes, well they're always sending people to the electric

chair. I must say that I'm jolly glad that we got rid of capital punishment in Britain before I was appointed to the Bench. Don't think that my conscience would have allowed me to deprive another human being of his life. And, of course, the trouble nowadays is that you never know when the police are telling lies."

"Sssh!" said all the others.

"I remember one of the men I sent off to be hanged," put in Sir Peregrine. "Many years later they found out that he didn't commit the murder at all. Someone else did."

"And did that worry you, Sir Peregrine?"

"Not at all. You see, by then I'd been promoted to the Court of Appeal."

"And what would you have done if you'd had your doubts about whether he did it or not? Transported him to Australia?"

"Oh no. They stopped doing that in my grandfather's time. He reckoned that in his day he transported so many convicts that they would have filled more than a dozen ships. Women and children too. He always believed that they'd be better off in Australia — away from their families and the criminal influences of home.

After he retired he went out to Australia in a sailing ship to see how it was all going out there. He used to stand with the flogging officer of the chain gang and watch all the convicts building the roads. Some of them he recognised as being the young men whom he had sent out from his court. "That is one of mine," he would say to the flogging officer. There was one gang that was building the road up to the Blue Mountains and every one of them were ones whom my grandfather had sent out. He wrote home and said that if it wasn't for him there would never have been a road between Sydney and the Blue Mountains.

But after about seven years some of the prisoners were given their manumission — you know, like the slaves in ancient Rome. After they'd worked for a master for a number of years they were allowed to go free. Well, one day my grandfather went into this butcher's shop in Sydney to buy some fishing bait and he recognised the butcher as being one of these manumated types whom he had transported. So he said, 'I remember you. I sentenced you to transportation for stealing that load of bread.' And the butcher didn't like being reminded of it in front of his customers so he grabbed his big butcher's knife and hacked my grandfather to death. Now that wasn't very nice, was it?"

"What? To embarrass the butcher in front of his customers?"

"No, to kill my grandfather."

The Treasurer picked up his silver fob watch to look at the time. "I'll give them until seven. If they're not here by then we'll go in on our own, say Grace and get on with our meal. I've been told by the chef that the game pie that he's cooked is truly delicious. And what year did you say the port was?"

"It's a thirty-nine."

"Eighteen thirty-nine or nineteen thirty-nine?"

"Nineteen thirty-nine."

"Ah, a very good year. The year I took silk."

■
———

Instead of being served game pie and vintage port in the elegant surroundings of the Inns of Court the Florida judges and their wives were forced by circumstances to eat at a fast food bar that served overpriced, tasteless burgers and soggy, undercooked chips — all presented in brightly coloured, non-biodegradable throwaway containers that polluted the environment in much the same way that their contents polluted the insides of those who were foolish enough to eat them.

The driver was waiting in the cab — pleased to be rid of his loud passengers for a while. At least until they returned and spread their "greasy food" breath throughout his vehicle.

The brightly painted hamburger bar was manned entirely by a team of smiling, positive looking teenagers who were the only staff that the management could attract since anyone of greater maturity would be far too embarrassed to hand such vulgar, tasteless, mass produced junk food to their fellow citizens. Indeed, the skills of the chain that sold all this rubbish lay in marketing rather than cooking. But none of this worried the Punchers and the Terracottas who were regular patrons of greasy food joints in Florida. They ordered three hamburgers each and double helpings of chips.

After stepping outside and wading through the sea of litter on the footpath the two couples made their way back towards the cab. They were about to cross the second intersection — which was, in fact, a fiveways — when the street lights went out. The normal eight-hour shift back at the power station had just ended and the workers for the next shift couldn't get through the traffic to take over. Everything went pitch black and the moon was nowhere to be seen. There were faint lights shining from one or two of the stranded cars but most drivers preferred to sit in the dark rather than risk running down their batteries.

"Which way did we come?" asked Terracotta.

"We turned at the house with a poplar tree in its front garden," put in the observant Lurlene.

"A great help!" exclaimed her husband scornfully. "In this light we wouldn't be able to distinguish a poplar tree from Father Christmas."

"Don't mention Father Christmas."

"Why not?"

"Next thing it'll snow."

"Oh, how lovely!" said Firma. "I've never seen snow."

"Well, if my memory serves me correctly, we made a turn from that road on the left."

"The first or the second one?"

"The first one, I think. We'll try it anyway. If the cab driver's got any sense he'll keep his lights on."

They made off along the dark street with their arms out in front of them. And they were singing *The Yellow Rose of Texas* at the top of their voices to indicate their presence to anyone who might be walking the other way.

They walked and they walked and they walked. But they couldn't see a taxi with its lights on. For the simple reason that they had taken the wrong turn. They realised this after half an hour and tried to go back. But a hundred yards on they came to a fork in the road and took another wrong turn.

"I think we're lost," said Terracotta. "We might never find the goddammed taxi. And I didn't even take his number. Did you?"

"No."

"I hope you didn't leave anything valuable with him. You've got your passport on you?"

"Yes. And Lurlene's too. There's only our case of clothes and I guess that, if the worst came to the worst, we could buy some new ones at one of their flash stores. Oh Christ! I've just remembered! My camera's in his bloody boot."

"You could replace it with the insurance money."

"Yes, but not what's inside it."

"What? Did you smuggle a bit of cocaine over here for one of your rich, white collar criminal friends at the country club?"

"No. The camera's got film inside it. All the shots that I took at the electrocution. One chap with his mouth open in agony just as the bolt of electricity hit him. I was hoping to win the big prize in the photo competition with it. Since I'm only an amateur photographer the prize money would have been tax-free. Damn! There goes ten thousand dollars."

Lurlene Puncher began to cry. "Oh come on," said Terracotta. "It's only money. My late father told me that you should never cry over money."

"I'm not crying about the money," wailed the sixteen stone District Attorney. "It's Hamilton!"

"Who's Hamilton?"

"Her golliwog. It's in her case in the taxi. Had the thing since she was a kid," said Puncher. "She can't get to sleep without it being tucked in beside her. It's so much a part of her that she

105

even carrried it on her wedding day. I had to give my vows first to her and then to Hamilton. The thing was even wearing its own little wedding suit."

"I'll never be able to get to sleep again in my life," sobbed Lurlene. "I'll just have to die."

The next thing she felt was the long, furry tail of a fox that brushed against her black stockinged leg. She let out a piercing scream and wondered what on earth would happen next.

The poor woman was now in such a state that her husband decided to seek a warm place for her to sit down rather than suffer her traumatic loss on the cold footpath of an unknown street in a strange city with not even a street light for comfort.

They could hear some loud rock music coming from one of the vehicles in the line of stationary traffic. It was about ten yards in front of them.

Puncher led them in the direction of the sound. It was emanating from a psychedelically painted minibus that belonged to a young musician who had driven up from Cornwall to attend the Grateful Dead concert which he now realised was outside the realms of possibility.

Judge Puncher banged on the doors at the back of the van. The volume of the music was turned down. Then the left door was opened by a young man with long brown hair, a moustache and two pairs of brightly coloured beads around his neck. He was wearing a pair of torn jeans, sandals without socks and a thick woollen Arran jersey. An aroma of incense wafted through the door from the inside of the van.

"Excuse me," said Puncher," but could we sit inside your van for a little while? My wife is in a state of distress and we seem to be lost in the dark. We're from Florida and I've only been in this country since lunch time and we haven't even got to Central London yet."

"By all means. It'll be a bit of a squash because there are already four of us in here—but we'll manage."

They helped Lurlene's sixteen stone frame into the vehicle. Then Firma. Puncher and Mohawk Terracotta brought up the rear and the owner then closed the door.

"Anyway, I'm 'Magic'," said the young man as he held out his hand.

"You're what?" exclaimed Terracotta.

"Magic."

"Then I guess we're in for an interesting time. Tell us some of the things you can do. For example, do you think that you could use your magical powers to unravel this goddammed traffic jam?"

"No, I don't mean that. I mean that I'm 'Magic'. That's my name."

"Are you 'Mister Magic' or is 'Magic' your Christian name?"

"It's my Christian name."

"And what is your surname?"

"'Mushroom.' But you can call me 'Magic'. I only use my surname when I sign cheques. And let me introduce Hester, Juliet and Anita." The three girls smiled. "We were on our way to Wembly Arena when we got caught in this jam. We were obviously fated not to get there so we're just making the most of it and enjoying our evening sitting here listening to the music."

"You're enjoying it!" exclaimed Terracotta.

"Yes. There's nothing we can do about it so we just accept it and make the best of it. No use complaining. It would only upset the complainant and do nothing to help the situation. I've already made use of my time and written a whole song in here this afternoon. Called 'Traffic Jam'. Do you want to hear it?"

"Not now. Maybe later," said Puncher. "My wife is in a state of distress and acute grief and might not be able to stand listening to a song about a traffic jam."

"Why? What happened? Did she trip over in the dark?"

"No," sobbed Lurlene. "I've lost Hamilton and I'll probably never see him again. We'll never find him in all the traffic."

"Who's Hamilton? asked Hester. "Your son?"

107

"No, her golliwog," said Puncher. "Had him since she was three. Never been to bed without him."

"And do you have any children?"

"No."

"I'm not surprised," thought Magic, "if she goes to bed with a golliwog."

"We're judges from Florida," said Terracotta. "We're over here for this law conference."

"And if we don't reach Central London by to-morrow," said a worried Lurlene, "then I won't be able to give my little speech to the Judges' Wives' Association."

"What's your subject?' asked Mohawk Terracotta. "The criminal tendencies of golliwogs?"

"No. The subject of my address is 'How to Promote The Death Penalty In Your Neighbourhood'. It's in the wives' own interests to push it at every opportunity — at church meetings, in country clubs, over the back fence, everywhere. Otherwise there won't be enough criminals for their husbands to send off to the Chair. I know that if Hiram doesn't kill at least one of them every month he gets ever so stroppy. And then it's the wives who suffer — having to put up with grumpy and unsatisfied husbands. That's why it's in their own interests to promote the death penalty and to try to have it extended to other offences as well.

I've spent every evening for the last three weeks preparing the speech and I'll be broken hearted if I can't get there to deliver it. Or worse — if I manage to make it but all the other wives are still caught in the traffic jam. Oh, the ups and downs of professional life! And to think of all those wretched prisoners on Death Row getting *free* meals at the taxpayers' expense." She resumed her blubbing while Magic made an attempt to change the conversation.

"Is this your first visit to Britain?" he asked Judge Puncher.

"No. I came over here a few years ago for a conference. An international society for which I was the American delegate."

"What conference was that?" asked Magic politely.

"International Society for the Promotion of Humane Techniques of Torture."

"That must have been fascinating."

"Yes, it was. Met lots of interesting people from other countries — Russia, Romania, East Germany, Iraq, Iran, Uganda, Zimbabwe, China. The most impressive speaker was a Frenchman, Monsieur de Guillotine. Charming chap. Been in the business for years. Well dressed too. The creases in his trousers were as sharp as a cutting edge."

"And what's it like to be a judge?" asked Magic who was beginning to wonder if it was all for real.

"Stressful at times. You know — complicated cases, sending them off to the electric chair, all the liberal claptrap we have to put up with from journalists, the hate mail, the death threats. That's why we've got six rottweilers guarding our house and, in my armoury behind the dining room, I've got just about every gun that you can buy in the state of Florida. Anyone who steps on my property will be shot dead without any questions being asked. Even a kid retrieving a ball. How do I know he's not a human bomb sent to harm Lurlene and me? Yes, it can be very stressful at times."

"But you don't have to be a judge, do you?" said Magic. "Everything in life is a matter of choice. That's why I'm a musician; I choose to be."

"But it's his career!" blubbed Lurlene. "And I'm in the law too. I'm District Attorney for an area with the highest crime rate in the state. They're all criminals; that's why we have to have the rottweilers."

Terracotta decided to change the subject. "We popped out of our taxi and went off for a hamburger and on our way back all the lights went out and we don't know where the hell we are. We could be in Timbucktoo."

"Well, how are you going to get back?"

"Haven't a clue in the world."

"You're welcome to spend the night in the van. There's no

way I'd turn you out in the cold. Maybe in the morning you'll be able to find your taxi," said Magic who, with his genial and easygoing nature, had no bad feelings for anyone — not even a psychopathic murderer like Puncher.

"That's very kind of you," said Terracotta. "Sure we're not intruding? Do you always travel with three young ladies?"

"No, not usually."

"To-day's a lucky day, is it?"

"Not really. I left Marilyn and Anna down in Cornwall; I could get only four tickets for the concert."

"You must be very tired."

"Yes, I think it's time for some kip." He began to arrange a mattress and some cushions on the floor and then pulled back the front seat to make a bed for himself and the girls.

"You won't all fit on there, will you?" said Puncher who was used to Lurlene's sixteen stone plus rolling around with her golliwog on their large, electronically alarmed double bed back in Florida.

"No problem," said Magic with a broad grin.

Puncher was looking at the girls. "Don't you ever eat? You're all so thin," he said. "Like that English model a few years ago — what was her name? Miss Thin Branch or something."

"Twiggy."

"Yes, that was the one."

The four overweight guests bedded down on the floor at the back of the van and tried to get to sleep. Before nodding off, the judges reflected on their change in circumstances. "And where should we be at the moment?" asked Puncher.

"In our suites at London's newest and most luxurious hotel after dining with all the lords and judges at the Inns of Court."

"And where are we instead?"

"In the back of a cold van with a bunch of bloody gypsies after the worst meal of hamburgers and chips that it has ever been my misfortune to force down my throat."

"I want Hamilton," blubbed Lurlene.

Chapter Nine

Humphrey Granville-Gore remained on the nineteenth hole longer than usual. One of the club members, a millionaire tea-bag tycoon, had scored a hole-in-one with the result that the Hole-In-One Fund was ripped open to pay for everyone's drinks. It was the first hole-in-one on the club's links since a country doctor had performed the same feat back in 1948. Not surprisingly, the Fund was a veritable Golden Calf and everyone was hell-bent on drinking it dry lest it might be another forty-two years before it was opened again — by which time at least ninety per cent of the present membership would be lying in a permanently horizontal position beneath the oaks and yew trees of country churchyards.

Humphrey always lingered on the nineteenth hole. Apart from its warm and convivial atmosphere the nineteenth gave him the chance "to keep in touch with the feeling in the shires". At least that is what he always told his wife when, upon arriving home several hours after dark, he was sometimes asked if the golf links were floodlit. But not-day.

Twenty minutes before nightfall Humphrey said good-bye to his fellow golfers, handed the head of his great-grandfather to the lady behind the bar to wash, and then drove back to his manor which stood in a thousand acres of pasture and woodland.

His wife was in the glasshouse planting seeds in boxes for the coming summer. Humphrey watched her for a few minutes and then spent some time screwing the handle back on a watering can. They heard the telephone ring inside the house. Mrs. Granville-Gore ran to answer it.

"It's for you," she said when she returned. "It's the B.B.C. They want to interview you about some traffic jam in London. I told them that you don't like being disturbed at week-ends." But her husband didn't hear these last words. He was bounding into the house to pick up the receiver.

"Her Majesty's Secretary of State for Transport here. I understand that you want an interview."

"That's right, sir. For the Six O'clock News."

"But it's already twenty to six!"

"Yes."

"Where are you now?"

"I'm speaking to you from London but our helicopter is already on its way down to drop in on you. It should have just crossed the border into Devon by now. You don't mind if it lands on your front lawn, do you?"

"No, so long as it steers clear of my wife's glasshouse. She's spent all the afternoon putting seeds in for the summer and it would break her heart to lose them. We'd have to buy our vegetables."

As he put down the receiver he heard the distant drone of the chopper as it came in from the east. Soon there was a deafening roar above the house as it positioned itself to land — carefully avoiding Mrs. Granville-Gore's tomato and cucumber seeds.

"But you've never been interviewed live before," exclaimed his apprehensive wife. "You'll have to be very careful what you say."

"Nonsense. It'll be a breeze. The only reason why I've never been interviewed is because Transport is such a backwater. Nothing ever happens — except motorway signs. Every time the murdering beasts in Northern Ireland kill one of our soldiers you always see the Secretary of State for Northern Ireland on the box — and sometimes the Defence Minister as well. Whenever there's a hostage crisis you see the Foreign Secretary. If inflation goes down — or up — by a point you see the Chancellor. Well, now it's my turn. Thanks to this little traffic incident in London."

In the beam of the helicopter lights Humphrey and his wife could see the technicians unrolling coils of wire and pulling cameras out of their cases. The interviewer, Cretin Borshead, came over and introduced himself.

"By Jove, you chaps were quick," laughed Humphrey. "I haven't even had time to change out of my plus-fours. I've just come in from golf. If you give me five minutes I'll go and change into a suit."

The interviewer, whose initials "C.A.B." were reputed to stand for "Cad And Bounder", could sniff both mischief and scandal in the air. A paid-up member of the Labour Party and a keen supporter of every left wing cause from the violent Mandelas to the Sadanistas, Borshead always derived a perverse satisfaction out of destroying Tory ministers on the screen.

"No, no, minister. You're fine as you are. You look homely and it is good to be seen as a sporting type. The British are a sporting race. They'll like it. And it'll lighten the atmosphere and lessen the drama of the traffic jam. It will also show that you are not panicking. A calm hand is just what's needed at the moment. And if ministers can't shine in times of crisis in their departments, then they'll never shine. In my humble opinion the sight of you on the box in your plus-fours will pull at least a million doubtful rural votes to the Conservative Party at the next General Election."

"Well in that case we may as well get started," said Humphrey as he led the team into the morning room and sat down in an armchair in front of the glass cabinet containing all his golf trophies.

"Such a good background!" exclaimed the interviewer. "Who knows, you might one day become the first golf playing Prime Minister since Mister Balfour."

"Yes, but at the moment I'm perfectly happy to be the Secretary of State for Transport and I declare that the Prime Minister has my full loyalty and support."

"That's what you all say, minister. If that was true we'd never have a change of leader."

The television set was on in the corner. When the News came on at six the man in the studio began by describing the traffic; then aerial shots were shown of the clogged streets. "And now from his country home in Devon is the Secretary of State for Transport." Click. Cretin Borshead gave his subject a slimy, reassuring smile and then began the questions.

"Tell me, Minister, how have you spent this day of unprecedented crisis? Have you seen the traffic at first hand?"

"No."

"Why not?"

"Because I've been playing golf all day down here in Devon. And, as you know, Devon is a long way from London."

"We got down here in forty minutes in the helicopter," retorted Borshead.

"Mind you, I have been kept fully informed of the situation by my office and early this afternoon I issued a number of directions for dealing with the congestion — things like ringing church-bells and lighting fires."

"Is there any truth in the rumour that you ordered all of Hampstead Heath to be burned down because you had an argument in Cabinet with the Minister of the Environment about pushing one of your proposed roads through a daffodil field in the Lake District where Wordsworth used to write his poetry? So you decided to destroy a big chunk of the Environment Minister's portfolio by burning down the Heath?"

"About as much truth in that as to say that television interviewers such as yourself know who their fathers are."

"Would you accept that the Government is responsible for the traffic jam by its failure to build new roads?"

"The Government is most definitely responsible....." — Borshead could hardly believe his luck — "..... for the large number of cars that have clogged the streets of London. By lowering taxes and making everybody more prosperous my Government has enabled people to buy cars who, under Labour's crippling taxes, couldn't afford them. And those who already had a car have been able to buy a second one. Rising affluence, Mister Borshead. The traffic jam is the crowning success of the government's economic policy. Nothing less than Britain's display to the world of its new found wealth. Every citizen driving an expensive car. It's the ultimate triumph of democracy. Ten billion pounds of shining metallic wealth exhibited on the streets of London.

Different from Russia where nobody can afford a car — or even a joint of meat — except for the Communist Party elite who grab everything for themselves and treat the rest of the population like dirt. Our traffic jam is the price we have to pay for living in a free, prosperous society. If you don't like traffic jams, Mister Borshead, then I suggest that you go and live in Moscow. No traffic jams there. No meat or bread either."

Borshead was distinctly put out. It was not going at all well for him; so he opted for a straightforward, functional question in a desperate attempt to regain the upper hand.

"At what time were you first informed of the chaos by your office?"

"I'm not sure what time it was but we were on the fourteenth hole and I was putting for a birdie. And the nation will be pleased to know that I got it."

"So you then rushed into the clubhouse and rang your office to tell them to burn down Hampstead Heath?"

"No, we finished the round of golf."

"You what!"

"Finished the round. Just like Drake finished his game of bowls before going off to defeat the Armada. And he was a Devon man like me. I don't know what part of the kingdom you come from, Mister Borshead, but in Devon we finish our games first and then deal with national crises."

"Do you think that it is appropriate for the Secretary of State for Transport to be playing golf on this of all days?"

"Well, I didn't know that there was going to be a big traffic jam, did I? After all, there are traffic jams in London every Saturday."

"And who is to blame for that?"

"Not me."

"Then whose fault is it?"

"King Charles the Second and his ministers."

"Charles the Second!"

"Yes, Charles the Second."

"The king who came after Charles the First?"

"Yes, but there was Cromwell in between. I did get a First in History at Oxford, you know."

"Pray, Minister, perhaps you might like to enlighten the British nation as to why to-day's traffic jam is the fault of a king who has been dead for more than three hundred years?"

"Gladly. When most of London was burned down in the Great Fire of 1666 Sir Christopher Wren designed a new road system to replace all the narrow gimcrack lanes that had proved so combustible in the Fire. The main feature of Wren's plan was a great wide avenue extending on an east-west axis from Saint Paul's all the way to the Royal Exchange; there were many other wide avenues leading away from it in all directions. It was almost as if Wren could foresee the era of the motor car.

Unfortunately Charles the Second and all the small-minded jacks-in-office of the time rejected this grand plan and insisted that the City of London be rebuilt exactly as it had been burned down so that every little pudding maker and baker could rebuild their shops and houses as before instead of being re-sited on wider roads. That's why we have all those ghastly narrow streets and no decent flow of traffic such as we would now be enjoying if Wren's plan had been adopted. I keep a copy of Wren's plan in my office in Whitehall......"

"Why do you keep it in your office, Minister?"

"So that, if ever we have another Great Fire, I can implement it straight away. Saves us the time and the cost of commissioning a new plan.

As I was saying, I have this plan and I can assure you that, if London had been rebuilt to Wren's design, then to-day's traffic

116

congestion would never have occurred. As I understand it, the worst congestion was in Central London — near the Thames bridges — the very area that Wren dealt with. The whole thing is the fault of Charles the Second and his ministers for so foolishly rejecting Wren's ideas.

As you are no doubt aware, Mister Borshead, they don't have such dreadful traffic problems over in Paris, do they? That is because, in the time of Louis Napoleon, they developed plans similar to Wren's and built all the great boulevards to carry the traffic. But here, we are still paying the price of Charles the Second's timidity and short-sightedness.

Speaking as a Low Churchman, my own view is that our Merry Monarch had too many mistresses. They would have distracted him from giving his full attention to Wren's master plan."

"Too many mistresses?"

"Yes."

"Well, speaking again as a Low Churchman, what would you say is the ideal number of mistresses that a man should have?"

"Depends whether he's a Low Churchman or a High Churchman. From my own observations and experience it seems that two is about the right number for a Low Churchman whereas most of the High Churchmen I know tend to have three. Not always in the same town, of course."

"And what about Broad Churchman?"

"Many more; after all, they're more broad-minded, aren't they?"

"Thank you, Minister, and before we go I would like to wish you a pleasant round of golf next time you play. Are you playing again to-morrow?"

"Yes. I'm in a four that's teeing off at nine o'clock."

"Do you know that the traffic jam is now expected to last well into Sunday and that hundreds of thousands of Londoners are going to have to spend the night in their cold cars miles from their homes and loved ones? Have you got a message for these people?"

"Yes. If they had heeded my advice and taken note of the church-bells and the fire then a lot of this nonsense wouldn't have happened."

"Thank-you, Minister, and I'm sure that every stranded motorist wishes you a successful round of golf to-morrow and hopes like hell that you fall in a bunker and never come out again."

Chapter Ten

When the soccer supporters emerged from the grounds into the fading light and traffic clogged streets they were not at all happy at finding themselves stuck in some of the most boring suburbs of outer London and miles away from their usual drinking holes.

A way out of the dilemma seemed to present itself when Smartie Artie, a regular footie supporter who had consumed a bottle and a half of Highland Mist since 9 a.m., announced that he would drive everyone back to Central London. In a train! He had once been a locomotive driver in Scotland and knew that, if only he could find a train, he would be able to work it. In the depths of his hazy mind he reasoned that, in spite of the closure of all the Tube stations, somewhere down there there must be a train.

The first step would be to smash through the metal grill across the station entrance and go down and have a look. That part of it would be easy; they always took some acetylene torches to the football. As well as sledge hammers, crowbars and knives. And, once they found a train, Artie would be able to drive it to any station in London. There would be no danger of a collision since they would be the only ones on the line. Artie would be the hero of the club. On a par with the player who scored the winning goal in the last minute. They might even make him a Life Member.

"Anyone got an acetylene torch?" he called. Several supporters pulled the equipment out of their bags and made their way to the grill. It took only a few minutes to break it down in key places and then they were able to slide the whole thing across to the other side.

119

A great cheer went up from the fans who had no idea where it was all going to lead but were quite happy to follow the leaders regardless. In any case, they enjoyed the sight of public property being vandalised—even if it was only a London Transport station grill.

A mighty surge of people passed through the entrance, jumped the turnstiles and ran down the stationary escalators to the platform far below. But there was no train.

"No problem," screamed Artie. "We'll walk along the track until we find one. Probably at the next station."

Like the Pied Piper, Artie led his faithful followers into the dark bowels of the earth. Some of them had torches and others just put their hands out in front of them as they ventured into the unknown — all the while singing their club songs and swigging whisky from their flasks. Some of the old geezers had had so many hundreds of alcoholic Saturdays that their bright red noses provided a further source of illumination. The one with the brightest snout was nick-named "Rudolph The Red Nosed Reindeer". This particular piece of wit brought a communal roar of laughter that reverberated and echoed right through the tunnel.

The first problem arose about two hundred yards along the line when the rails suddenly split into two and forked off in different directions. "Which way shall we go? Anyone got a Tube map?" Again they all roared with laughter.

"Can anyone else drive a train?" asked Artie.

"Yes," came a reply from way down the line. "One summer when I was between jobs I did a stint driving the Romney and Hythe for the kids down in Kent." They all roared again.

"Do you think you could manage a big train?"

"Of course!" replied Roundhead. "The bigger the better."

"Right then," called Artie. "You go that way and, if you find a train first, drive it back here and then turn down this tunnel and come and collect the rest of us. We'll push on this way and, if we find one, we'll drive it back here and collect you lot. Easy."

Of course it was easy. There were only two ways to go so

half of them followed Artie while the rest went with the hero of the Romney and Hythe miniature railway.

Artie's lot made it to the next station but there was still no train. Just an empty platform which they vandalised as much as they could before moving on again through the darkness in the direction of the next station.

Unfortunately Roundhead and his party had unknowingly made their way along a service tunnel that went down and under the Tube lines until it surfaced for the first time at a mainline station some eight miles ahead. It twisted and turned and forked and undulated so much that, after about half and hour, one of the more sober among them came to the chilling conclusion that they had taken so many forks and turns that there was no way of going back the same way that they had come.

"I think we're lost," he called out. "It's like being down one of them great coalmines in Yorkshire — you know, the ones that they've been working for hundreds of years and there are passageways off in all directions and, unless you have a map of the place, you'd be lost in five minutes."

"Yes, but it's easier to get everyone out of a coalmine," screamed one wit. "All ya've gotta do is get Mister Scargill to call 'Out' and everyone will be out in a couple of minutes. Usually for eight months."

They came to a side tunnel and some of the laggers went to investigate. It was narrower than the main tunnel and there were no rails on the ground. One of the more observant noticed the difference and concluded that it must be an escape route for drivers who might lose their trains and therefore it would lead up to the safety of the street. Some of them already had visions of popping up out of a manhole and emerging in some busy road to the cheers of all the shoppers and pedestrians. And so it was that the last six men of the column decided to follow this new tunnel and steal a march on their comrades who were already another fifty yards along the service tunnel.

These six brave men christened themselves "The Hooligan

121

Half Dozen" as they walked along the ever narrowing tunnel that sometimes rose and sometimes fell and sometimes curved but never seemed to end.

During a rare interlude of silence they heard some noise ahead. Footsteps? No. More like a scratching sound. It was starting to grow louder when they felt the first of the big, healthy rats run up and down their legs. Five of them tucked their trousers into their woollen socks to keep the blighters on the outside but the sixth of them, Hamish MacBrayne, was not so lucky. He was wearing a MacBrayne kilt and, in true Scottish tradition, there was nothing underneath. The rats were running up his legs and starting to nip him in vital parts. They were everywhere — even jumping down from the roof of the tunnel. The men turned round to go back but soon found a triple fork and were at a loss to know by which route they had come in.

"Well," grimaced the uncomfortable Scotsman, "if there are rats we must be getting near the top. Ye ken, they feed off all the rotten vegetables outside greengrocers' shops and all that sort of thing." In spite of the heavy aroma of alcohol that surrounded them they noticed that the smell was definitely becoming stronger. And the rats were getting bigger. And their tails longer.

Then the batteries in their single torch went on the blink. A couple of minutes later they failed altogether. The two men up front put their hands out ahead of them to feel the way. They took two steps forward. The others followed. They walked a few more yards — still with their arms out in front of them. It was so dark that they couldn't even see the floor of the tunnel which was a shame as it suddenly stopped and gave way to a twenty foot vertical drop into a huge subterranean chamber that was filled with the most filthy and foul smelling substances known to man. They were no longer in the London Underground but were floundering around up to their necks in the London sewer.

Their fellow travellers, under the inspired leadership of the former driver of the Romney and Hythe miniature railway, didn't have to walk the whole eight miles of the service tunnel. After five and a quarter miles one of them noticed a hole in the roof with an iron ladder rising up vertically into what seemed like an eternal blackness. By climbing on the shoulders of the others one of the more agile among them pulled himself on to the bottom rung and began climbing. About eighteen rungs up he could see a tiny speck of light far above him. As he got a bit higher he noticed that it was peeking through what was obviously a crack at the side of a manhole.

"We're saved!" he cried to the eighty or so others who began climbing up behind him.

The glimmer of illumination came from a powerful electric light that shone over the front entrance of Scotland Yard. The duty "plod" was about to go off shift. It had been a most trying day. The traffic jam, his football team had lost, the horse he backed at Cheltenham had come in last and, to top things off, all the passers-by had laughed at him and asked why the hell the police hadn't been able to "unjam" the traffic. The last thing he needed was an army of drunken netherworld creatures to pop up out of a manhole and start making rude comments.

"Good evening, officer. Seen any good horror movies lately?"

"What's the weather been like up here? Been as hot as hell where we've come from. But now that we've been reincarnated we'll try to behave better in our new life. We don't want to return down there. Too hot! And too many men with pitchforks and big red ears."

"Is Queen Victoria still on the throne? We've been a bit outa touch down there."

"Say, Mister Plod, I sure like your uniform. Will you come dancing with me to-night?"

It was now seven o'clock and Artie and his men were still gallivanting from station to station on the Central Line. But they hadn't yet found a train.

An hour earlier the train drivers had called off their strike and announced that all services would resume running at seven o'clock. And they did.

Artie and his merry men were midway between two stations when they heard a distant roar above the din of their singing. It seemed to get louder very quickly. But they couldn't see it coming as there was a sharp curve in the tunnel. And, of course, the curve prevented the driver from seeing them until he was right upon them.

He applied the emergency brakes but it was too late. The front of the speeding train was already mowing down the football supporters and chopping them to pieces with its wheels.

When the emergency services arrived they shone their bright lights on the mangled bodies and torn scarves that were strewn all over the floor of the tunnel. It was not a pretty sight. "I guess that's what Passchendaele must have been like," said one of the young medics with a sigh.

Chapter Eleven

When Myles arrived back at Aston Square he was greeted on the stairs by Fiona who had returned half an hour earlier from her journey to the Mall. "Oh Mylo, you should have seen the traffic. All those poor people sitting in their cars all day with no hope of moving!"

"I know. I saw them as I rode past on the A40."

"What were you doing on the A40?"

"Driving the Prime Minister to Chequers. Pillion."

"Oh that's not fair! You won't take me on a run with the Angels and yet you take her."

"It was an emergency. She had to meet the President of France and her own people didn't seem to be able to do much for her. It was my national duty."

"So the nation comes before little old me?"

"Sometimes it has to, my love. By the way, did you go to Portobello Road?"

"No, my agent rang up and I had to do a commercial instead. Annabelle went on her own."

"And did she buy the chastity belt?"

"Oh yes. She's already tried it on upstairs and guess what?"

"It doesn't fit?"

"Oh, it fits all right. Only too well. Problem is, she 's already lost the key. We've been searching everywhere for it. You see, it's locked and she's wearing it."

"Let's continue the search to-morrow," suggested Annabelle as she came down the stairs. "It's probably a good idea to wear it to the party to-night. Without the key."

"What party?" asked Myles.

"Oh Mylo, we forgot to tell you. The girl from whose stall Annabelle bought the belt, well her name's 'Pixie' — she's part punk and part acid head. Well, she went to school with Annabelle and she told her in the greatest confidence about this super acid house party to-night down in the East End and guess where we have to meet and when?"

"Outside Stratford Station at midnight."

"How did you guess?"

"The Angels are going."

"That's all the more reason why I want to go! At last I'll be able to meet them. I mean, I'd be safe with them in a party of a thousand people, wouldn't I?"

"Guess so. But I've got this wretched brief to read. Look how thick it is."

"All right, if you want to be a bore and not come, we'll go on our own — won't we, Annabelle?"

"Too right!"

"Very well, we'll all go. And I'll just stand up in court on Monday and say 'I'm sorry, your Honour, but I haven't read the brief because I went riding with Hell's Angels on Saturday afternoon and attended an acid house party in the evening'."

"Why don't you say that the reason why you haven't read the documents is because you had to drive the Prime Minister around as part of your national duty?"

"You're the one who should be the barrister," he laughed. "You're far quicker than me."

The telephone rang. "It's for you, Mylo," said Fiona as she handed him the receiver.

"That you, Myles? Uncle Douglas here. I'm just ringing to thank you so much for that rugby ticket. Most exciting match I've ever seen. A real cliff-hanger right to the end. I mean, you can't get it any closer than 28-27. It was the highlight of my trip.

By the way, were you at the match?"

"No, I couldn't make it. Too much work. Was it a good seat?"

"Couldn't have been better. Just above the ten yard line. I sat next to another farmer. He has a sheep run a few miles out of Cape Town. Found we had a lot in common so we had a drink in the bar afterwards. He's asked me to visit him when I go to South Africa which is the next leg of my trip."

"And where are you now? Back at your hotel?"

"Good God, no. I've only got as far as Richmond. Walking you know."

"And what's the traffic like out there?"

"I wasn't going to mention the traffic as I didn't want it to appear that I was being critical but may I ask you just one question?"

"What's that?"

"Is it always like this on the roads after a rugby match?"

"No, to-day is something exceptional."

"You see, where I live in inland New South Wales you hardly ever see another car on the road. And if you do, then you usually stop and have a chat. I've never seen a traffic jam before and what I've seen today has just about blown my mind. Do you think that they'll ever clear it or will all those people have to spend the rest of their lives sitting in their cars and reading the number plate of the car in front of them?"

"God only knows!"

"I don't think that even He would know how to fix it. Now, how can I get from Richmond back to my hotel in the West End? I don't reckon I can walk that far."

"I just heard on the radio that the Tube has started running again. Take a District Line from Richmond; that'll get you back to Central London."

"Well, thank God for the Underground. I'm flying out on Monday and so I would deem it my pleasure to treat you and your young lady to dinner at my hotel to-morrow night."

127

"That's awfully kind of you. We'd love to come but unfortunately I've got a brief for Monday and I haven't even looked at it yet. And we're going to a party to-night and won't be home until to-morrow morning. May I ring you at lunchtime and say 'Aye' or 'Nay'? Of course, we'd love to come and I know that Fiona is dying to meet you but there are certain times when pressure of work prevents me from leading a normal life."

"I know what it's like. Come shearing time and I was always so flat out that I didn't know if I was Arthur or Martha."

"All right, we'll talk to-morrow."

"And thank-you so much for the ticket."

"Pleasure."

He put down the 'phone and turned to Fiona. "That was Uncle Douglas. He wants us to have dinner with him to-morrow night at his hotel."

"Ooh, that sounds nice."

"But what about the brief? When am I going to get a chance to look at it?"

"Try to-morrow afternoon. I'll go out shopping with Annabelle and we'll leave you in peace for three hours."

"Yes," he thought sarcastically. "My brain should be in top form by then. Right after an all night acid house party."

■
———

They watched the Television News at eight o'clock and Fiona "oohed" and "aahed" at all the amazing pictures of the traffic. Aerial shots of the endless lines of cars were broken by close-ups and interviews with some of the affected drivers.

The most distraught was a woman from Chelmsford who claimed that she had "just nipped into London to see some friends off at the Airport" and then couldn't get back to feed her twenty-two cats, fourteen dogs, eleven hamsters, eight guinea pigs and pet baboon, all of whom, she claimed, now faced imminent malnutrition and might have to be put down. "She's the one who should be put down," scoffed Myles. "Imagine having that menagerie as your next door neighbour!"

There followed interviews with numerous pregnant mothers and elderly women who had each been promised a cash payment of a hundred pounds if they would collapse into tears in front of the cameras. They all obliged admirably with the result that there was a greater proportion of the News taken up with the shedding of tears than the uttering of words.

However, the best television fare of the evening came after the News; it was billed as a "debate" between a couple of representatives of motoring organisations and two of the loony councillors who had voted for the closure of the bridges and tunnels.

All four participants had to pass through metal detectors before they went on the screen and the resultant confiscation of several metallic weapons meant that the ensuing melee was confined to fisticuffs. There were no Marquis of Queensberry Rules and no boxing gloves either. It was a straight hand to hand encounter that would have done credit to the great bare knuckled prize-fighters of yore like Tom Spring and Tom Cribb.

The contest started with some vicious words that developed into physical blows in the first few minutes. The motorists' leader struck a powerful punch in the left eye of one of the councillors who then began pummelling his attacker in the ribs. The two men grappled together and fell down fighting.

The camera zoomed on to the other two combatants who were chasing each other around the stage with the wooden chairs that had been placed at the table for the "debate". Crunch! The councillor brought it down on the bald, shiny skull of his opponent. Before the shock of the blow had time to register the victim enjoyed a split instant of superhuman strength during which he struck back a mighty blow beneath the jaw. The motorists adopted a wide range of scientific punches whereas the councillors, both ex-security guards with a penchant for violence, went for non-stop, heavy hitting. They punched each other both right and left and the highlight of the evening was when some blood from a burst artery shot on to the lens of the camera. "And we believe that one of the councillors has now been punched insensible," panted the excited commentator.

"What a load of rubbish!" exclaimed Myles. "As if the fellow was ever sensible in the first place."

During the sixth round one of the councillors, who was not unlike King Kong in appearance, grabbed his attacker in a headlock and dealt out the punishment mercilessly. The man took it all and then used his teeth to bite the councillor as he delivered yet another blow. The councillor screamed and loosened his grip whereupon the other escaped, ran round behind him, and felled him to the floor with a tremendous blow to the head which felt like the impact of a sledge hammer.

After eight bruising rounds the exhausted interviewer declared it a knock-out win for the motorists who seemed to be suffering almost as many fractured bones as the losers. An air ambulance landed on top of the television studio to ferry the four participants to Saint Bartholomew's Hospital where a team of anaesthetists and orthopaedic surgeons was on hand to receive them. When the end of the fight was announced some ten million viewers let out a howl of disappointment and immediately switched to the other channel that was showing a blood and guts Western.

Chapter Twelve

In the dimly lit basement of the "Nothing, Nowhere, Never" coffee bar in Soho four young men and a woman were sitting around a low table drinking Viennese coffee out of clay mugs. The men were dressed entirely in black — shirts, trousers and leather jackets — while Matilda looked almost as dull and colourless in her loose fitting grey slacks, soiled cheesecloth top and brown leather jacket. There was a wall around their alcove on three sides and, since it was only 8.30 p.m., they had the whole place to themselves.

Ben was the oldest of the group. With his long, dark, greasy hair that fell to his waist and a skull and crossbones tattooed on his forehead he looked more than a little intimidating to the man in the street. But not to the others at the table. He had been kicked out of the army after punching his platoon sergeant on the nose and since then he had never had a job. Nor did he have a proper house. Like the others at the table he lived in "squats". None of them saw any reason to pay rent when they could move into someone else's house which might be empty. As anarchists they did not believe in private property or the right of any individual to own property or even to keep others out of his house.

For years they had discussed all sorts of theoretical ways of destroying the government and all the structures that keep society together but in a practical sense their achievements had been nought. But they did sometimes use a spray-can late at night to squirt anarchist slogans on railway bridges and the sides of concrete buildings.

Unlike some other anarchists, whom they had met at protests and demonstrations, these five had never joined any of the anarchist societies. To do so would compromise their principles and make a complete mockery of their opposition to all forms of organisation — even a society of anarchists. In short, Ben and his friends were the hardest of hard core in the shady world of anarchy. And, in their eyes, the traffic chaos that now prevailed on the streets of London was a God-given opportunity to create mischief against their sworn enemy, the State.

Ben had already tried to start a revolution during the afternoon in Trafalgar Square. There had been the usual crowds there doing the usual things: old ladies feeding the pigeons, men sitting on the benches reading their newspapers and young teen-agers scaling the statues of the lions and sitting atop their manes while sucking on the end of a beer bottle. What was different was that there was no traffic noise or movement. The great square was completely surrounded by several lanes of motionless taxis, buses and cars and even a great caged truck carrying a circus elephant. All the motorists were still sitting in their vehicles — reluctant to leave just in case God came down from Heaven and cleared the traffic.

Ben overheard a few of the old ladies saying how nice it was to be able to feed the birds without having their senses assailed by an endless parade of filthy, noisy vehicles. It gave him an idea. He gathered all his friends into a group in the middle of the square and they started chanting, "No more cars! No more cars!" Other members of the public, surveying the chaotic standstill that had been caused by the internal combustion engine, took up the cry. "No more cars! No more cars!"

The motorists interpreted this as an attack on themselves and their metallic possessions and decided that, on top of every-thing else, this really was the last straw. So they got out of their cars, noticed the hundreds of vehicles that were clogging Whitehall and Northumberland Avenue in an effort to get to the blocked bridges, and chanted back, "No more councillors! No more councillors!"

Ben could hardly believe his luck. "It'll soon be like the Winter Palace when the Tsar was brought down," he had whispered to Matilda.

"No more government! No more government!" screamed Ben and his friends. But it didn't catch on. The people resumed feeding the pigeons, reading their papers and guzzling their beer while the motorists got back in their cars and turned on their radios in the hope of hearing news of their deliverance.

Despite this little setback, Ben remained full of hope. "It's definitely the best chance we've had since the fall of the Tsar to bring about a collapse of the system," he crowed as he went to take another sip of his coffee.

"But that didn't do our cause much good, did it?" put in Matilda. "Look what followed — a rigid communist state in which tens of millions of people were murdered and the rest of the population were treated as slaves for the next seventy years."

"Yes, but this time we'll keep the state of anarchy going. As soon as there's a breakdown of order we'll make sure that no one will ever be able to put it back together again."

"Do you really think that the British people would stand for that?" asked Paul, who was a little more sceptical than the others. "If you ask me, it's the most stable society in the world. They've never had a Revolution like in France and Russia; nor a complete breakdown of the state as has happened in Germany every now and then. Hell man, Hitler bombed London for more than a hundred nights in a row and they never even looked like cracking. They're bloody stubborn. There's no one else in the world like them. And they thrive in adversity. Like in a traffic jam. Seems to bring out the best in them. That's why they win every war. Hell man, I was walking through Hyde Park this afternoon and what do you think I saw?"

"Hordes of people at Speakers' Corner getting ready to march on Parliament and smash the State?"

"No. Young men of the Household Cavalry riding their beautifully groomed steeds along the sand track and carrying on

133

as if nothing unusual was happening. Just as they have done for hundreds of years in the past and will probably do for hundreds of years in the future. That's the type of thing we're up against.

We're not talking about some jumpy Third World structure like the Philippines. One decent traffic jam in Manila would be enough to bring their government down. And, if they didn't clear it by the next day, the second government would probably fall as well. But not in London. I really can't see the British state falling to pieces just because there's a traffic jam — much as I'd like it to!"

. "Just makes it a bigger challenge for us," said Ben defiantly.

"Anyway now that the Tube is running again," continued Paul, "people will be able to move around. Even though the traffic is still jammed they'll nevertheless be able to make the most important journeys — on the Tube. They'll just carry on under difficulties — like they did in the Blitz. Hell, if Hitler and all his thugs couldn't dislodge them, how do you think that the five of us sitting around this table can do it?"

"We might not be able to bring down the State but we can still inflict some wounds," continued Ben. "As I see it, the Tube is the key to the whole thing. If it is only the roads that are blocked, then — as you say — people can still use the Tube. But if both the roads and the Tube are unusable — like they were to-day — then the authorities are in real trouble. And we have it in our power to bring the Tube system to a complete halt."

"How?"

"By lighting small fires at the stations." The others' eyes lit up. Pyromaniacs at heart, they all loved lighting fires.

"And what is more, the ensuing chaos will be a result of the government's own stupidity. Remember the King's Cross fire?"

"Too right!"

"Well, in their usual belief that a mere piece of legislation is the panacea for all ills, the authorities over-reacted — as they always do when they've got the newspapers on their backs. And so they brought in a whole shaft of regulations in the aftermath of the fire so as to lock the stable door after the horse had bolted and it is these very regulations that will be their undoing.

The rule now seems to be that, even if there is the smallest fire on a Tube platform or anywhere in a Tube station, they have to close the station, stop the trains, call the Fire Brigade and then the firemen have to go all through the station checking this and checking that and, of course, nothing can move until the fire chief gives the all-clear. That's why there are always so many delays at Tube stations. Before the King's Cross affair, if someone dropped a match on a fish and chip paper on the platform and it caught on fire, the station staff would just smother it out. Now, they have to report it to the Fire Brigade, close the station and all that.

So, all we have to do is go round lighting small fires on the platforms and they'll stop all the trains and ring the Fire Brigade; the stations won't be able to reopen until they receive the 'all-clear'. But the fire engines won't be able to get through the traffic and so there'll be no 'all-clears'. And the trains will be stopped indefinitely. All because of our little fires and their own legislative over-reaction to the King's Cross fire."

"Brilliant! When shall we do it?"

"Well, I'd like to think that operation could take place on Monday morning when everyone is trying to get to their work." They all giggled at the stupidity of people who had to go to work instead of shoplifting their way through life like they did.

"Do you think the jam will last until then?"

"Oh yes. And if we wait until Monday it'll give us time to ring Wolfgang in Hamburg and Steve in Amsterdam to bring all their crowd across and give us a hand. They can fly here with all that money they've just pinched. And the more people we can muster, the more fires we can light and the more chaos.

I'll ring our Hamburg and Amsterdam friends from that 'phone box in Earl's Court which we discovered doesn't need coins. That's if I can get a place in the queue. They should get here by to-morrow and we'll be able to light the fires at strategic stations at seven on Monday morning and have the whole Tube system at a standstill within thirty minutes. The commuters will be stuck in dark tunnels for hours. Maybe even days if it takes that long for the fire engines to get through the traffic."

They toasted the coming platform fires with the dregs of their coffee and then made their way up to the street where they faded into the dark night and returned to their various squats.

Chapter Thirteen

Myles, Fiona and Annabelle decided to travel to the meeting point at Stratford by Tube so as to avoid the continuing chaos on the roads. They took the last train of the night going east and knew that, by the time they would be ready to come home, the Sunday morning services would be well under way.

"Oh, this is so exciting!" enthused Fiona as they stood in the crowded train that was filled with happy football drunks, irate motorists on their way home from their stranded cars and young acid heads on their way to the party. Outside Stratford station thousands of excited party-goers were hiding in lanes and shop doorways in an effort to conceal the true size of the crowd that had gathered. They always took such precautions but to-night it was hardly necessary; on a day of such extremes and disorders a large number of people walking together along the footpath would barely raise an eyebrow. Not even at midnight.

"I love a mystery," exclaimed Fiona, " and there is no more thrilling mystery than going to a party and you don't know where it is."

The marshals waited until the last of the general public had drifted away before leading their excited flock through dimly lit streets, over a high wire fence, through a small stream and across a bomb strewn paddock towards a darkened warehouse.

"It's like a bloody obstacle course," scowled Myles as he rolled up the legs of his trousers to wade through the freezing, muddy waters of the stream.

"Acid house parties are always difficult to get to. Haven't

you ever been to one before?" asked Fiona.

"No. They haven't yet become the big rage at the Temple. And you?"

"Yes, I went to a couple of them last year when I was doing some modelling work up in Manchester."

"And what were they like?"

"Super. That is until the police came and ripped out all the sound equipment and started threatening and arresting people. Some of them were real coarse types— especially the younger ones. So different from the nice, peaceful party-goers. Until the pigs came no one laid a hand on anyone. At least not in violence; only in love. There must have been five hundred of them — all wielding their truncheons and with fire and envy in their eyes. And it was four o'clock in the morning! You'd think they'd be out trying to catch all the burglars instead of smashing up peaceful parties. I mean, they hardly ever seem to catch burglars, do they?"

"Too hard for them," scoffed Myles. "Don't forget, they're not the brightest bunch."

"Do you think they'll come tonight?"

"No way. They wouldn't be able to get their cop cars and paddy wagons through the traffic and so they wouldn't be able to arrest people and throw their weight around. That'd take all the thrill out of it for them."

Inside the warehouse it was all flashing lights, loud acid house music, endless energy, bright clothes, shining jewellery and tripping couples. A world in itself. Such a contrast to the darkness outside and the misery of a million frustrated motorists still sitting in their cars or trudging home through the cold.

It wasn't cold in the warehouse. At the far end was a great fire which the Angels were feeding with loose boards, old chairs and any other combustible material they could find.

"Hello Myles!" called Jackal as he saw his fellow rider enter the building — followed by Fiona in a pink luminous dress and Annabelle who was wearing a black and white zebra striped outfit with the chastity belt underneath. "I thought you said that

138

you weren't coming, Myles."

"That's right but I was talked into it by these two."

"Gee, Myles, you're a real dark horse. Keeping a couple of spunks like these all to yourself. Me and the boys, we've been walking around and looking at the structure of the place — you know, how it's fitted together so that we can knock it down in the shortest possible time. Maybe get our photos in the Guinness Book of Records. Demolition time is 7 a.m. You'll wait round for that, won't you?"

"Too right. I haven't been to a decent demolition party since last New Year down in Cornwall when we took some pianos down to the beach and smashed them to pieces."

"How many?"

"Six. Including two grands."

"Look, there's Jasper!" cried Jackal. "He's the one who's putting on the party. The owner of the building — well, at least for the next few hours. Until it comes crashing to the ground. Hey Jasper, come over here and meet Myles and all his spunks."

The owner, who was wearing a leopard skin suit with a bow-tie of flashing lights, came over and shook hands.

"Myles is a barrister when he's not riding with us," said Jackal by way of introduction.

"Splendid!" exclaimed the happy host. "Just what we need. We've now got a doctor, an engineer and a lawyer. Nothing can go wrong. The doctor can attend to any injuries, the engineer can supervise the demolition and, if the pigs should launch one of their pathetic raids, you can emerge as our leader and get us all off the hook."

"No way," said Myles. "I'm off duty to-night. And I'm here for one purpose only and that is to have a good time."

"There is no other reason for anyone to be here," laughed Jasper as he cruised off to greet some more of his guests.

"Oh, look! There's the Metal Man!"

Myles looked up and was temporarily blinded by the

wildly spinning coloured lights that were shining on the arms, legs and trunk of Lloyd Mitchell-Emery, the Metal Man.

Six and a half feet tall and with a shining shaved head, the Metal Man was invariably the first sight that greeted the eyes of arriving guests at London's warehouse parties. He was always in the same rig: chain mail vest, a solid rounded silver piece—rather like an inflated loincloth—that covered his vital parts fore and aft, while his arms and legs were totally enclosed in approximately four hundred bangles that ranged in width from a three inch copper monster that was studded with rubies and emeralds to thin bands of silver and gold.

To-night he had a six inch long sharp, pointed rod protruding horizontally out of his left ear lobe with the result that anyone who was foolish enough to kiss him would probably finish up with a large amount of blood on their face.

To attract further attention he was carrying a large silver fan which he kept waving high above his glistening, shaved head. He had even stuck luminous green tape to its curved outer side so that he could be seen in the dark.

The old Cockney lady who cleaned his flat had put in some overtime polishing him up before the party with the result that he shone like the Golden Calf. It was always his proud boast that he wore one and a half times more metal than the armour clad Richard the Lion Heart when he rode off to the Third Crusade.

Every morning the Metal Man pored over the pages of the Financial Times for the latest prices on the London Metal Exchange in an effort to ascertain his current worth. Some days he went up; other days he depreciated.

"Pity he wasn't around in 1940," said Myles cynically. "He could have made a significant contribution to Lord Beaverbrook's campaign for scrap metal to build more Spitfires." They all laughed. "I just wish I'd brought my sunglasses."

"Well, at the moment I think he's being attacked by Messerschmitts," laughed Fiona. A cascade of laser beams were homing in on the shiny surface of the Metal Man's exterior decoration. Flashes and visual explosions rebounded off his chain mail vest and bangles and it really did look like a dog-fight in the skies above southern England— circa 1940.

"At least he'll be happy," said Myles. "He always is when he's the centre of attention."

When the laser attacks ended the Metal Man re-emerged in one piece (or, to be more accurate, four hundred pieces if one included the bangles) and the dancing resumed.

"Let's dance," said Myles. "I want to get into the swing of things."

"Me too!" cried Jackal. "And do you know something? These acid heads aren't nearly as bad as we thought. I've just signed one of them up for the chapter. Now I'd like to dance with one of your ladies."

"Take Annabelle. She's the one who's wearing the chastity belt."

Myles and Fiona danced through the next seven numbers. Totally mesmerised by the glamorous and mind-bending atmosphere of the party. All around them were good looking young people in stylish clothes and exotic jewellery — all dancing, touching, kissing and jumping up and down to the wild music. Some of the partygoers were wearing fluorescent gloves that shone in the darkness as they waved their hands through the air.

Half a dozen young men, clad entirely in purple and looking both wide-eyed and dangerous, were gliding from group to group. They had purple hair and were carrying purple water pistols in purple holsters. In return for a small consideration in the form of a five pound note these dream merchants would aim their converted water pistols and shoot small "purple hearts" into the open mouths of the eager guests.

The fast dance music was in the hands of a Manchester band, The Twelve Foot Faces, whose incredible energy on the stage set the pace for everyone else.

Far above them in the high pitch of the roof was a large loft-like floor which had once been used for storing sacks of grain.

Now the only means of access was up a long wooden extension ladder. From time to time some of the guests went up it; other times they came down. And sometimes those going up met those coming down and they all had to climb over each other.

"Let's go and see what's up there," suggested Myles. They waited for a couple, who were dressed as snakes, to slither their way down. They then began scaling the rungs. The higher they went, the hotter the atmosphere. The heat of the Angels' fire was starting to settle inside the pitch of the roof. It was so hot on the platform that most of the guests had taken off their clothes and were dancing naked. A fair skinned young man was going around with a tray of water paints and daubing great stripes down people's bodies while his girl-friend showered them with glitter.

One girl was completely orange; her partner green on his front and yellow on the back. A dancer from north of the Border had his clan tartan painted on his chest while his girl-friend, wearing only a shell necklace, was coated entirely in silver and sincerely believed that she was a mermaid for the night.

Another girl, who claimed to be Lady Godiva, was complaining that she had lost her horse whereupon a chivalrous public school boy obligingly got down on his hands and knees and let her ride him like a jockey.

"What a party!" gasped Fiona as Myles unzipped her pink dress which fell to the floor. He then kicked it on to the big pile of clothes at the side of the platform. It was so hot up there. And ever so sensuous.

"We're in a world of our own in this place," said Myles. "It's like being inside a spaceship and spinning round the earth."

"Do you think that they'll have commercial space flights in our life-time? I'd really like to go up near the moon and see what it's like."

"Perhaps. But it would be very expensive. And anyway, how would you deal with the weightlessness?"

"I couldn't feel any lighter than I do now."

Boom! A smoke bomb exploded. Then another. And

another. From their elevated position they could look down and see the thick white cloud slowly rising. Soon they were inside it and no one could see more than a couple of inches in front of them. "Hold me tight, Mylo. I'm scared of getting lost and falling over the edge." He ran his hands down her neck and over her smooth, soft buttocks before drawing her tightly against his own throbbing body. As he did so he felt the fingers of Lady Godiva wandering over his bare back; in the confusion of the smoke bomb she had lost her public school boy as well as her horse.

It took ten minutes for the smoke to clear. The first person Myles saw after he loosened his grip on Fiona was Barmaid Betty who had a mad clown painted on her back by a young art student. "I'm the new sign for the Mad Clown," she whispered to Myles. "They're going to hang me out from the gable. Do you think I'll draw the customers?"

"Yes, so long as you don't put any clothes back on. Then nobody would be able to read the sign."

"But *I'm* the Mad Clown!" interjected Josh Hayward who was all decked out in a red and white striped clown's suit, thick white lipstick and a clown's hat with a bell on its pointed top.

"You're a particularly well-spoken clown," said Myles. "You're not a barrister by any chance, are you? In real life, I mean."

"What's real? No, I am not a barrister but, like them, I do make my living out of my voice."

"So you're the town crier?"

"No, but you're getting hot. I read the News on the television."

"So you do!" exclaimed Fiona. "You're the nice one who always says 'Fri*day*' instead of 'Fri*dee*' like all the others."

"What is the point of speaking English at all if you don't aspire to speak it properly? Now, I must be off. I've got a lot of partying to do before I read the News at ten-thirty to-morrow morning."

Everyone resumed dancing. "I wonder how Annabelle's

getting on with Jackal," whispered Fiona.

Annabelle in fact was getting along very well with Jackal; the only problem was the key. The Hell's Angel was beginning to see himself as a Crusader in a suit of shining armour, riding his horse towards his maiden only to find.......that he had lost the bloody key. Jackal led her outside and tried all his bike keys but none of them fitted. Nor did his house key. The other Angels all offered their keys but to no avail.

"There must be some way," uttered an exasperated Jackal after nearly an hour of trying more than a hundred keys. "Surely some of the Crusaders who went to the Holy Land must have sometimes lost their keys during their battles with the Turks. Perhaps we should put a request over the loud speakers for a locksmith."

"No one would hear; there's too much noise," said Annabelle. "The key is back at Myles' place — somewhere. We should be able to find it when we get back."

"I can't wait until then," cried Jackal. He looked at the stolen watch on his wrist. It was 6.30 in the morning. "Hell, I'll have to go and round up the boys for the demolition party. And we'll have to move everyone down this end. We're knocking the far wall down first. Then the roof and the platform in the middle and then this end. By that time everyone will have moved outside and will be keeping warm in the blaze."

"What, are you going to burn it all down as well?" exclaimed Annabelle.

"Too right. Fire's our specialty. To-night we've even got the permission of the owner."

"Is he paying you to do it?"

"No, it's our pleasure."

"What about the engineer? Isn't he going to direct you?"

"No, he's too out of it. That's him over there; the one with three girls on each arm. I wouldn't want to disturb him."

He stood for a moment staring up at the roof. "Wait here. I've got to go up the ladder and clear the decks. Don't want to burn

144

anyone. Not even acid heads."

He climbed up the rungs and nearly fell off when he reached the top and saw all the naked, brightly painted flesh.

"Clothes on everybody! All down! Fire about to start!" he roared above the sound of the Twelve Foot Faces.

With natural grace and style and without hurrying the dancers put on their clothes and came down the ladder in dribs and drabs. When the last man touched the ground the Angels, with all the discipline of a bomb disposal squad, lowered the ladder, cleared everyone away from the far end and began knocking the place to pieces with sledgehammers and chain-saws. The owner was delighted. "It would cost me ten thousand pounds to have it done professionally and professionals wouldn't do it as well as these boys."

Pieces of the wall and roof were thrown on to the fast spreading flames which brought hundreds of rats scurrying from their hiding places. The air was filled with the sound of shattering glass, chain-saws in full cry, the cheers of the party-goers and the strains of the Twelve Foot Faces who were still struggling to be heard above the rest of the din. By now everyone was outside and standing a safe distance from the action. They were kept warm by the heat that was being thrown out by the fast spreading conflagration. Already the warehouse was clothed in a bright orange glow that reached up into the dark, moonless sky.

The flames rose to the roof of the building; twisted beams cracked and moved and eventually came crashing down. The loft hung perilously as the posts supporting it were being steadily devoured by the fire. One post was already burnt right through but still the loft held. A second post went as everybody watched in breathless anticipation. Suddenly another post gave way and the whole structure fell down with a deafening bang.

The tremendous vibration of the crashing loft activated the high explosive bursting charge of an unexploded bomb that had been lying about a foot under the soft ground outside the back of the warehouse ever since it was dropped by the Luftwaffe in 1940.

All the explosives stacked inside its metal casing burst out in one massive, simultaneous emission. What remained of the warehouse was blown to kingdom come and one of the Angels got his hand burnt.

The night was now so bright that every detail of patterned clothing, intricate jewellery and hand-painted body designs could be seen with great clarity. Everything, that is, except the key to Annabelle's chastity belt which remained as elusive as the Loch Ness monster.

The bomb blew a crater in the ground and pierced a water main that carried the water supply to that part of East London. The great fountain of water that sprayed up from beneath the ground glistened in the bright orange glow and produced a surreal spectacle that added a whole new dimension to the wondrous acid trips that several of the guests were still experiencing. The Metal Man clanged his way to the rear; he didn't want to rust.

No one knew where the bomb had come from and some of the acid heads were so confused that they began hurling rocks in the air to deter further imagined German bombers.

Eventually the huge spray of water had the effect of dousing the flames and dampening the fire; the fresh smell of burning wood was replaced by the foul stench of damp smoke. The amazed partygoers had to put handkerchiefs over their noses and mouths as they stood there gaping at the dying flames and remains of the warehouse in which they had spent the last few hours dancing, tripping and kissing.

"That was a much better show than Guy Fawkes Night," exclaimed Fiona.

"Yes," replied Myles, "and if the Angels had been around to help Guy Fawkes, there's no way he could have failed to blow up Parliament,"

"And would that have a good thing or a bad thing?"

"Hard to say really."

■
———

It was 10 a.m. when they returned to Aston Square—
Myles, Fiona, Annabelle and Jackal. The Tubes were unseasonably full for a Sunday morning and at least half the passengers were clutching prayer books and hymn sheets. And on the roads above
— which had been *slightly* cleared during the night — the church traffic was now pulling out of garages and driveways which ensured that any improvement in the situation during the night would be only temporary.

The Cardinal Archbishop of Westminster, not wanting the collection plate money to be down, had appeared on television to remind his flock that a mere traffic jam was no reason for good Catholics to miss Mass on a Sunday morning while the Archbishop of Canterbury, comfortably ensconced amidst all the gold and crystal of Lambeth Palace, had decreed it a Day of Special Prayer and urged everyone to make a special effort to go to Matins to pray for an end to the traffic jam. And so, as a result of these sacred but misguided exhortations, the traffic remained jammed for another day.

However, none of this worried the occupants of Number 18 Aston Square as they sat around the kitchen table drinking coffee and discussing the party, the fire and the bomb.

Fiona started to yawn. So did Myles. "We're off to bed," said the master of the house. "You two can do what you like as long as you don't disturb us."

"Before you go, Myles, can you get me something?" said Jackal.

"What?"

"A magnet."

"There's one down in the garage. What do you want it for?"

"To find the key, of course. It must have fallen on the carpet so I'll go round all your floors with the magnet and try to suck it up."

"And if you don't find it?"

"I'll probably have to use an acetylene torch."

Myles returned with the magnet and then dragged himself upstairs to the bedroom. Fiona was already in bed. He walked to the bedside table and began setting the alarm clock.

"What are you doing that for, Mylo? I'm so tired I want to sleep until Monday morning."

"I have to get up at two o'clock to start work on the wretched brief. And I promised to ring Uncle Douglas to tell him whether or not we can make it for dinner to-night. Of course, the answer is 'No'."

"How long do you think the traffic jam will last?"

"Goodness only knows. Shall we turn on the telly to see what the experts have got to say?" But Fiona had already drifted into the world of dreams. Myles was still a little too alert for sleep so he grabbed the remote control and turned on the box for the Mid Morning News.

Josh Hayward had pulled the top of his clown's suit down to his waist and replaced it with a white shirt and tie and dark grey jacket to read the News. He didn't bother with the trousers because he knew that the camera never went below the base of his chest. He began in serious vein as he rattled off the facts and progress (or rather lack of it) of the Great Traffic Jam. It was, he said, "the largest traffic jam in the history of the world, there were an estimated million and a quarter cars still stranded on the streets of the capital but — hallelujah — there hadn't been a single road fatality in Greater London since Friday night."

"Police chiefs have used the traffic jam as a pretext to ask the Government for special powers to control the movement of people and cars but a Home Office spokesman has told them that the British people didn't fight two World Wars just to be bossed around by a Fuhrer in a police uniform."

"Quite right," said Myles out loud. "They've already got far too many powers over our lives. Damned cheek they've got to ask for more."

Josh Hayward continued reading the News with a grave expression on his face which he found harder and harder to maintain in view of what he had consumed at the party. "The police say that they have the situation fully under control and have banned to-day's VW Beetle car club rally from Birmingham to London for fear of creating a tail-back all the way from Central London to Spaghetti Junction."

It was the word "Spaghetti" that caused him to crack up. He couldn't restrain himself any longer and fell into fits of laughter. Then, with a great effort to regain control, he held his breath in for a few seconds and turned the page to read the next item of the News. "Control yourself, Josh," he ordered under his breath and then ventured into new territory.

"After a meeting of the Common Market Commissioners in Brussels it was announced that part of the Community's 'Spaghetti Slag-Heap' will be sent to feed undernourished children in....." He collapsed again into uncontrollable hysterics.

A late item was then placed on his desk by an unseen electronic hand that rose from a hole in the floor. "And an item just received says....that the traffic jam.....is now expected to last....until Mon...day." This time he went totally out of control. He rocked with laughter on his chair and finally fell off. The last things that the viewers saw were his red and white striped clown's pants that flew up in the air as he toppled off his perch.

Myles burst out laughing himself and so did thousands of other Londoners who were watching it from the comfort of their beds or armchairs. But it wasn't at all funny for the stranded motorists who were facing Day Two of their ordeal.

After they had woken and lifted their aching backs off the uncomfortable car seats, some of them went walking through the crisp morning air to buy a cup of hot tea and the Sunday papers.

The news made them even more miserable. "No hope of ever clearing it!" screamed one particular inch thick headline while page after page showed photos of sad looking people standing by their cars in the cold.

The strident and intolerant tabloid papers screamed out to their semi-literate readers that the government should "do something". That "something" included banning all cars from Central London, banning rock concerts at Wembley, banning crowds from going to football matches, banning the Springboks and even banning Saturday weddings on the grounds that they add to traffic congestion.

This authoritarian and simplistic approach went down well with the poorly educated masses who buy the tabloids. Lacking the broader understanding and tolerance of the better educated classes, the tabloid readers liked it simple and they liked it strong.

The puritanical editors and other self-appointed guardians of the public good now added the motor car to all the other things that they wanted banned — smoking, fireworks, fox-hunting, acid house parties, adult magazines and most other things that fun-loving and adventurous souls like to enjoy in their spare time.

The Daily Reactionary made its usual demand for "more police with greater powers". The editorial thundered that, if the Government couldn't find enough recruits to the constabulary, then they "should have enough guts to start enlisting Rotarians, scout masters and school teachers skilled in corporal punishment to make up the deficit and keep the unruly elements — like car drivers who get caught in traffic jams — in a state of constant fear."

And, of course, all those who were forever singing the praises of capital punishment, now had a new cause to thrash. "Three years' jail for double-parkers who block traffic!" was their war-cry. Since the main aim of these unpleasant types was always to inflict punishment on someone, somewhere, their goal was admirably attained. It was, in fact, the ultimate punishment for the hard-pressed drivers to have to read this sort of crap as they sat in their freezing vehicles wondering where it was all going to end.

The alarm clock sounded at exactly 2 p.m. Myles put his hand out to silence it and Fiona, who heard it in her sleep, dreamt that it was some sort of air-raid siren for the bomb that had gone off at the end of the party.

Without getting out of bed Myles leaned over and pulled the telephone towards him. He then dialled the number of the hotel in the West End where Uncle Douglas was staying. He was now wide awake.

"Mister Douglas Kingsley, please."

"One moment, sir."

"Hello, this is Myles. I'm awfully sorry but we can't join you for dinner to-night. I have to spend all the afternoon and most of the night on the brief. It's a particularly complicated one and I haven't yet thought out the correct line of argument."

"I understand even though I am disappointed as I was looking forward to meeting your lady. And I don't know when I'll be making another trip Home to England.

Now if you and your young lady ever feel the urge to come Down Under I'd be most honoured to have you to stay. I am, as it were, fairly well-known in my particular district and so you would get to meet all the other farmers. And we have some good wines in the Hunter Valley."

"Thanks. That would be great. Enjoy your flight to-morrow. And don't forget to take the Tube to Heathrow instead of a taxi. There's no way that the M4 will be cleared by the morning. At the moment you're safer underground than up top."

"Just like when I was last here. During the Blitz."

"How's the traffic in the West End?"

"Well, the cars are still all lined up in stationary rows outside the hotel. The dining room was full at lunchtime. All the people in the cars came in for something to eat. I've been up on the roof of the hotel taking photos of all the traffic in Piccadilly to show my neighbours when I get back. Otherwise they wouldn't believe me."

"Right. Well, have a pleasant journey."

He put down the 'phone and fell asleep again. Dreaming that he was sitting on the wide verandah of a wooden farmhouse in the Australian countryside, staring at endless paddocks of sheep and watching the orange sun go down over the desert. And he had a glass of rich, red Cabernet in his hand — from the Hunter Valley, of course. There was an old man sitting next to him who was wearing a brown leather hat with corks hanging down from its wide brim. And the man looked awfully like Uncle Douglas.

■
───────

On the next floor down Annabelle was asleep on the couch in the drawing room. Alone. After an hour and a half of searching the carpet in vain Jackal had finally given up. "Hell, I reckon you're a real spunk," were his parting words, "but I can't handle the obstacle course."

The peace and quiet of the house was shattered at 5.30 p.m. by a ring on the doorbell. Annabelle roused herself from the couch, wiped the sleep out of her eyes and dragged herself to the door. There were two people standing there in the rain — looking both distraught and miserable. The man introduced himself.

"Hello. I'm Tristan Bude-Blakiston. I'm in chambers with Myles. We came here one night for a chambers dinner party. And this is my wife, Hannah. As you can see, she's in labour and we can't get through the traffic to Saint Mary's Hospital where we've got a booking in the maternity section. We've been sitting in the car for nearly two hours and then I recognised this square as being the one where we came to Myles' dinner party last year. Is Myles in?"

"Yes, he's upstairs — asleep."

"Would you mind awfully if we came in to have the baby? And could you act as midwife?"

It was all too much for Annabelle. She opened the door to

let the anxious couple in and then ran upstairs to rouse Myles.

"Quick, Myles! There are some people from your chambers who are having a baby in the drawing room."

"What? Oh, come off it. Did you have some of that acid at the party last night? One micro-dot too many? Anyway, what's the time?"

"Five-thirty."

"Morning or evening?"

"Evening."

"What!" Myles almost hit his head on the top of the four-poster as he realised that he had missed the whole afternoon that he had set aside for reading the brief. He was dressed and downstairs in less than two minutes.

"Oh, hello Myles," said Tristan in the gravest of tones. "I can't tell you how happy we are to be here. Everything was going according to plan. I've arranged a babysitter for the other children, a booking at Saint Mary's and then we got caught in this wretched traffic and couldn't get any further. Hannah's been in labour for about half an hour and we really thought that she'd have to have the baby in the street — just like they do in darkest Africa.

We racked our brains to see if there was anyone we knew who lived in these parts and then I suddenly remembered your place from that wonderful dinner party we had here last year — you know, when old Sparrow-Pencarrow, Q.C. fell into the pavlova. You don't mind, old chap, do you?"

"Of course not. Listen, there's a nurse who lives across the square. I'll run over and fetch her. She'll know what to do. And what to bring with her. " Hannah Bude-Blakiston's groans and screams were getting louder. "I just hope the nurse is at home," called Myles as he ran out the door.

Five minutes later he appeared with the nurse who was in her jodhpurs, having just returned from a ride in Hyde Park.

"Listen," said Myles. "My bed upstairs is more comfortable than the couch. If Hannah can make it up the stairs, I'll rush up and throw some clean sheets on." The expectant mother nodded lethargically and was helped up the stairs by her husband and the nurse.

"Quick!" said Myles to the still sleeping Fiona as he started to pull the sheets off the four-poster. "Get up! Someone is going to have a baby on the bed."

"Who? Annabelle?"

"No. The wife of one of my colleagues. They can't get through the traffic to the maternity hospital."

"Oh good! I love babies," she said as she stood up and walked towards the *en suite*.

Fifteen minutes later Hannah was delivered of a healthy, bonny son who weighed seven pounds, nine ounces when they dropped him on the bathroom scales.

"Honestly, Myles, I don't know how to thank you," said the smiling, sweating father. "Far better than having it on the street."

"Yes, well this calls for a small celebration. Wait, I've got a little something downstairs. We'll toast the new arrival in champagne and welcome him to our world with all its modern wonders — including traffic jams."

He went downstairs, popped a bottle of Moët, poured its contents into six crystal glasses, which he put on an antique silver tray, and then walked back up to the room of safe delivery.

"Well, I just hope that all this trouble of finding somewhere to be born isn't an ill omen for his future," said the thoughtful father.

"I wouldn't let it worry you," retorted Myles. "The greatest men in history have had to be born in sudden, makeshift circumstances. Don't forget, Christ was born in a stable with an ox and an ass breathing over him to keep him warm and Churchill was born in a cloak room at Blenheim Palace during a ball. I think it's probably a good omen. Maybe he'll become a great man and save the world from some future catastrophe. Like a traffic jam."

"I hope you're right."

"How many children have you got now?"

"Five. Three boys and two girls. Oh, that reminds me, could I use your 'phone please; I want to ring Eton to put his name down. It's very tight now to get into the top public schools."

"Of course, use the one downstairs." Tristan hurried out of the room.

"You're so lucky to have had a baby," said Annabelle to the happy mother. "I love babies."

"Well, I'm sure that your turn will come," said Hannah, "and then you'll be able to experience the same pleasure that I'm going through at the moment."

"I'll never be able to have a baby."

"Why not?"

"Because we can't find the bloody key."

Chapter Fourteen

Inside the office of the Supreme Commander of London Traffic things were at last moving. At 6 p.m. Assistant Commander Dullard walked in with a big smile on his face to announce what he believed was the best news of the year — the councillors had just finished their emergency meeting and had announced that they would unblock all the bridges immediately.

"Our point has been made," they insisted, "and there is no further need for 'controlled congestion' to exist on the Thames bridges."

"The traffic should be flowing freely again within a couple of hours," said a relieved Dullard.

The Commander was in a mild panic. He and Slick Nick stood to gain more than two million pounds if they could spin it out until 11 a.m. Monday.

"It's not quite as easy as that, Assistant Commander," he said. "In my judgement, if these councillors are prepared to be so irresponsible as to block vital bridges then there's no knowing what else they might be up to. I think that this temporary 'ceasefire' on the bridges is nothing more than one of their Marxist ploys to lull us into a false sense of security to make it easier for them to execute their next move."

"What do you mean?"

"How do we know that the reason why they're putting all the traffic back on to the bridges is to obtain the maximum death toll for when they blow them up?"

The Assistant Commander looked stunned. "I'm sorry,

Dullard, but I won't have it on my conscience to let unwary motorists on to those bridges just to be blown to kingdom come by a bunch of loony left-wing councillors. I want all those bridges sealed immediately and checked by our security people to make sure that explosives haven't been planted anywhere on the structures. The search is to be under water as well as up top. That's an order."

"Yes sir. But if we're going to have police divers doing all that work, the bridges won't be functioning until to-morrow. There'll be a hell of a jam in the morning when everyone tries to get to work."

"Can't be helped. Anyway, even with these extra security measures, they should all be ready by about 10 a.m. The traffic should be flowing freely again by eleven. I can virtually guarantee that. In fact, so confident am I that you can ring the B.B.C. and book me on the screen for eleven o'clock to-morrow. Tell them that I've got an important announcement to make."

"And have you?"

"Yes. It will be the formal announcement of the end of the traffic jam."

■
———

By 7.30 p.m. the little nativity party at Aston Square was beginning to break up. The nurse, still in her jodhpurs, had just left for her own house but promised to return in a couple of hours. Annabelle had drunk six glasses of champagne and was flat out on the couch. The circumstances of the lost key having denied her one form of pleasure, she didn't see why she should be deprived of others — like champagne.

Tristan had gone for a walk to the corner to see if the traffic was clearing but returned a few minutes later with the news that his own car, which he had left in a stationary line a few blocks away, was still in exactly the same place with the same green Triumph Herald in front of it and the same pale grey delivery van

157

behind. "We're never going to get home to-night and, anyway, Hannah is probably not up to it."

"You can stay here," said Myles. "You and Hannah can sleep upstairs and we'll use the couch down here."

"What about Annabelle?" asked Fiona.

"Annabelle will just have to go home," said Myles. But that was easier said than done. The subject herself was virtually comatose and, since she lived on the other side of London, there was no way that they could send her off on her own. Or even put her in a taxi. "We're just going to have to walk her to the Underground, go with her on the train and take her to her own place," said Myles.

It was half past nine by the time they returned from their mission of mercy. "I'm sorry, Tristan, " he said as he walked in the door, "but I'm going to have to be unsociable; I've got this wretched case at the Bailey to-morrow morning and I haven't even looked at it. I'm going up to my study and reckon I'll be there for the next four hours. Fiona will talk to you and look after you and Hannah. The drinks' cabinet is over there. Make yourself at home."

But when he reached the second stair there was a power cut. Everything went black. And there was only one candle in the house and that, insisted the nurse, must be put in the bedroom because Hannah was about to feed the baby. And Myles knew that at that hour on a Sunday night all the shops were closed. And anyway there was now a pea soup fog outside. The only lights were the miles and miles of car headlights that filled the streets of London. But they could be seen only dimly through the fog. He knew that it would be pointless to venture out in search of candles.

When the power came on again Myles was asleep on the couch. He woke at 6.a.m. and decided to go straight to his chambers. He reckoned that, if he read the brief on the train and also for an hour when he arrived at chambers, he might become familiar enough with it at least to get through the first day of the trial.

Unfortunately he couldn't get a seat on the train and was squashed among a number of large overcoats (all of which had flesh inside them) which prevented him from being able to open his briefcase—let alone read the papers. He alighted at the Temple station a few minutes before the anarchists lit their fires which was to bring the whole Tube system to a halt for the rest of the morning.

When he reached the door of his chambers at the top of the winding, rickety staircase he put his hand in his pocket for the keys. But, having slept in the drawing room instead of the bedroom, he had left them on the bedside table in the latter and had forgotten to pick them up. "Damn!" he thought. "It's been a weekend of lost keys. First Annabelle's and now mine. I'll just have to wait for the clerk." But the clerk was deep in the bowels of the earth. On a stranded train.

Myles sat down on the top stair and began reading his brief. His only companion was the chambers cat, Elspeth, who was curled up in the corner, having just licked dry the saucer of milk that had last been replenished on Friday evening. For some reason which he had never bothered to analyse Elspeth always reminded him of a woman judge. "Only difference is that Elspeth's hair is a bit softer than the tough horsehair wigs that those old cows deck themselves out in," he thought as he ran his eye down the list of counts in the indictment.

A few minutes later he heard some footsteps at the bottom of the bare wooden stairs. He looked down and could see the top of a black bowler hat climbing towards his floor.

"Who's that?" he wondered. "No one in our chambers wears a hat — let alone a bowler!"

When the man turned on the last landing Myles was amazed to see that it was Julian Blatherstone, the youngest member of his chambers.

"Good morning, Julian. Have you got a key?"

"Yes."

"Thank God for that; I've left mine at home because I didn't sleep in my own bedroom."

"Why not? Too untidy?"

"No. Hannah Bude-Blakiston gave birth to a baby boy in my bed yesterday evening and I didn't feel like turning her out."

"Was it your baby? Chambers wife-swapping or something?"

"Good God, no."

"Then why was it born in your bed?"

"Tristan couldn't get her to the hospital because of the traffic jam."

"Don't mention the traffic jam to me!"

"Oh, all right. Tell me, what's the occasion for the hat? I didn't think that gentlemen wore them indoors."

"This gentleman does and he's not taking it off until he gets to court and puts on his wig."

"Why?"

"It's all because of the traffic jam."

"And is that how you got the punch on your snout as well?" asked Myles as he noticed a piece of white sticking plaster on the front of his colleague's nose.

"It wasn't a punch. It was worse. Two holes in the thing."

"That's funny," said Myles. "I've got two holes in mine too; they're called nostrils."

"Yeah, well I've now got four."

As Julian bent down to put the key in the latch Myles noticed that the usual golden curls that had always covered the back of his colleague's head were no more. He was shaved like a Buddhist monk.

"You didn't have a car accident, did you?" asked Myles. "Looks as if your head has been surgically shaved."

"I wish it was a car accident but unfortunately — as the radio keeps crowing — there wasn't a single motor accident in London on Saturday night."

"Well, what is it then?"

"Listen, Myles, I had planned to keep it a mystery but you're a pretty understanding sort of chap so I'll tell you what

160

happened or at least what I can remember of it — as long as you promise not to tell another soul. Couldn't stand the story getting round the Temple. It'd bring my career to an abrupt stop. Were you in the traffic jam yourself?"

"On and off. But I was on a motor-bike so I was able to get through."

"Well I wasn't. I got stuck in the usual Kensington High Street jam at 10 a.m. It normally clears by lunch time but not on Saturday. By one o'clock I was completely fed up and hungry and thirsty as well. I heard on the car radio that it wasn't expected to resolve itself for many hours. So I locked the Rover, left it where it was and headed for the nearest pub for a gin and tonic. Several other motorists were doing the same."

"What happened then?"

"I don't exactly remember but I obviously had far too much to drink. I can remember playing a game of darts with some punks and then I think I had some more drinks with them. There were two chaps with bright pink hair and three girls who were wearing torn black stockings and leather jackets. They were really funny and making me laugh like mad.

I remember asking them what it was like to have pink hair and rings through their ears and noses and they asked me if I would like to try it. Now everything after that is very blurred but I remember going upstairs to some market with them — like in an arcade. There were lots of stalls selling punk clothes and jewellery, a hairdresser, an ear piercer and all that sort of thing. In short I went in as a straight dude and came out a punk."

"I didn't know that there was such a place," said Myles, "where you could be transformed into a punk so quickly."

"Well there is and it's in Kensington. If you take my advice *never, ever, ever* start drinking on your own in Kensington. When they led me into this market place I thought I was in some sort of Arab casbah and that they were leading me to the harem; that's why I went along with them. Then everything went blank.

The next thing I remember was waking up in some seedy

161

basement flat at Notting Hill with a whole lot of punks around me wearing chains and leather. I thought I was having a nightmare. They all cheered when I stood up and welcomed me to 'the wondrous and carefree world of punk.' I was bursting to go to the toilet; when I got in there and looked in the mirror I nearly had an apoplexy, a brain haemorrhage and an epileptic fit all at once. Two silver rings through my nose, rings with razor blades hanging from them through my ears and the tiny shoots of hair that the wretched hairdresser had left on my head were luminous green. I've spent the rest of the week-end trying to wash it out but it's bloody stubborn and I think I'll just have to wait until it grows a bit and then cut it out. But that 'll only prolong getting my hair back to what it was before this frightful episode."

"What about the holes through your nose? What are you going to fill them in with? Putty?"

"God only knows. At the moment I haven't even got a place to live."

"No?"

"My wife kicked me out. When I eventually extricated myself from my erstwhile drinking friends I went back to the car; it was midnight and there it was still in the same place with the same black Austin Princess in front of it and the same red Royal Mail van behind it.

I walked all the way home to Wimbledon and Vanessa refused to let me in. When I explained who I was she just stood on the doorstep shrieking and said that if she'd wanted to marry a man with a bone through his nose she would have spent her youth husband hunting in the jungle of New Guinea instead of saving up to buy expensive dresses to wear to all the May Balls at Cambridge. And do you know what the most embarrassing part of it is?"

"No."

"The case I'm doing to-day at Inner London Crown Court; I'm prosecuting a group of punks who drank too much and smashed a shop window in the King's Road. Thank God I'll be wearing a wig!"

Myles couldn't control himself any longer. He burst out laughing. He couldn't stop. He laughed all the way to the Old Bailey.

When he reached the Central Criminal Court he was gratified to hear that most of the cases had been deferred because of the inability of vital participants to attend. But his relief was short-lived.

"Not your's, Mister Padstow," said the Clerk of the Lists. "You'll be pleased to know that everyone has made it — judge, jury, counsel and defendants and we'll be starting in ten minutes."

"Hello, Myles!" called his instructing solicitor. "Guess what?"

"Holy mackerel! What am I going to tell him?" thought Myles.

"I've just come from the cells below where I've been talking to the client; he's decided to plead guilty. So, it'll just be a matter of entering the plea and having the matter deferred for sentence until another day. Hope you didn't spend your whole week-end working on the case. Would have been a dreadful waste of time."

"Not the *whole* week-end," replied Myles with a smile.

"I hope you don't mind, but I'm going to have to leave you," said the solicitor. "I have to dash to Horseferry Road Magistrates' Court to defend one of these mother-in-law cases. Nearly every solicitor in London has got one this morning."

"What's a 'mother-in-law' case? I've never heard that expression in all the years I've been at the Bar."

"No, I don't suppose you would have — considering that they only started on Saturday morning."

"Meaning?"

"Myles, old chap, can't you work it out? A million people trapped in their cars for the best part of two days. A certain proportion of them were sons-in-law who had offered to take mother-in-law for a quick drive. To the pictures, to the doctor, to the psychiatrist, to the wig shop — wherever. They thought they'd have the old bat in the car with them for only half an hour or so; instead, they had to sit with her for two days!

My client says that he was asked a hundred and eighty-seven rude and nosey questions and on the hundred and eighty-eighth he cracked. There were a couple of window dusters on the dashboard so he stuffed them down her gob, tied her hands and feet together, got out of the car and locked her inside with the engine on. Then he blocked the exhaust pipe with his oil rag and gassed her to death.

There have been nearly a thousand of these mother-in-law killings since the traffic jam began. Most of them were strangled with the seat belts but some were bludgeoned to death with metal jacks and others were conned into drinking weedkiller. A few drivers who were alongside Hyde Park were able to impale the old girls on the spiky tops of the metal fence bars."

"Then it looks like the prisons will be full for the next few years."

"Nonsense. They'll all get off." And so they did. In the collective wisdom of all the street-sweepers, dole bludgers, wife beaters, illiterate immigrants, drunkards, nincompoops and others who sat on the juries the ordeal of having to sit in close confinement with one's mother-in-law for up to forty-eight hours was regarded as justification for any crime — including murder. In any case, they knew that there was no danger of the accused re-offending as, in the absence of bigamy, a man could have only one mother-in-law and, with her already dead, the crime could not be repeated.

Defence barristers merely had to stand up in court and say that their client was stuck in the Great Traffic jam of 17th to 19th February with no one else in the car but mother-in-law and it worked like a charm.

"Forty hours, members of the jury. Forty hellish hours of non-stop chatter, nagging, complaints, gossip, mischief-making, abuse, criticism, the old girl blowing cigarette smoke all over the car, asking him to put in her eye-drops, change her bandages, hold her false teeth. And then there were the questions.

'Why don't you shave off your moustache? Why don't you go home after work instead of spending your wages at the pub? Why don't you wear pyjamas in bed? Why can't you get a better job? Why did you put me on to that horse that came in last? Why did you send me that postcard of a dragon when you went to Hong Kong? Why did you get drunk and take off all your clothes at my seventieth birthday party? Why are you so selfish? Can't you do something about the weather? Why do you always drive me into a traffic jam? Why didn't you take me to Spain with you last summer? Why don't you listen to me when I'm talking?

When are you going to pay me back that hundred pounds I loaned you in 1965? Why did you send my measurements to the undertaker? Why did you send me a broomstick for my birthday? Why do you live up four flights of stairs when you know I've got a bad heart? Why do you always go to your parents for Christmas dinner instead of coming to me? Why did you put my death notice in the paper on April Fools Day? Why did you hire that man to run me over with his motor-bike?' It was at this point, members of the jury, that my poor client decided that he had had enough."

The jury understood; they put themselves in the place of the accused and wondered why he had waited so long before reacting. And so it was that every mother-in-law killer was acquitted and sent home with the good wishes of the jury.

■
———

The Commander's security staff finished their search of the bridges at 9.30 on Monday morning but Thicknesse delayed opening them for another half an hour. The traffic moved slowly at first as the drivers steered their cars on to footpaths and traffic islands to edge their way forward wherever there was a gap. Two way roads were made one way and it wasn't long before the traffic began to flow more easily.

The Commander looked at his watch. It was fourteen minutes past ten. His driver was waiting to take him to the B.B.C. studio to make his big announcement. "Such perfect timing," thought the Commander as he ducked his head to get into the car.

"Excuse me, sir. There's still massive congestion near Big Ben," said Dullard. "I don't see how you can announce the official end of it until this little problem is cleared up. Especially since it's in full view of Parliament and all the lobby correspondents who are always hanging around there looking for something to write about."

Dullard was right. The problem was that on Saturday afternoon a clamping unit had travelled the wrong way along the one free lane leading away from Westminster Bridge. Some motorists in the clogged lanes had laughingly called out: "Hey, where do you think you're going? We drive on the left in this country."

The creeps in the clamping truck — with about three and a half braincells between them and hearts as hard as the metal hoist which enables them to go about their sordid work — didn't appreciate being on the receiving end of a joke. Especially when three of the jokers were driving late model BMWs. There were only three sets of clamps on the truck. But that was enough. One for each BMW. Over the protests of the well-spoken, well-heeled drivers, the cowboys in the truck banged the hated clamps on each of the three cars. One in each lane. Where they remained for the next forty-eight hours. Deserted by their owners who had gone to their offices in the City to do some productive work.

"What's the problem, Dullard? Every bridge has been given the security 'all-clear'. Including Westminster Bridge. So why isn't the traffic flowing there?"

"There are three cars blocking three lanes and it seems that they can not be moved."

"Why not?"

"I don't know because I haven't had a full report yet.

Maybe they've broken down."

The Commander looked at his watch. It was now 10.25 a.m. And he knew that the journey to the studio would take at least twenty minutes. Plus another five minutes to travel up in the lift. "Which was the last bridge to be searched by the explosives team?" he asked.

"Westminster."

"And where are the explosives people now?"

"Waiting by the bridge for their truck to come to collect their gear."

"Very well, Dullard. Order them to place explosives under each of the three cars and blow them to kingdom come. Immediately."

"But sir......"

"Immediately, Dullard. Otherwise don't bother coming back to the office. There are plenty of other fish in the sea who would like a nice cushy office job like that of Assistant Commander."

"May I ask you your reason for such an extreme act?"

"Yes. I have grounds for believing that those three cars have been placed there by the I.R.A. They're time bombs just waiting to go off. Right by Parliament. If we don't hurry and blow them up under controlled conditions, they'll go off themselves and take the whole British Parliament with them. You don't want to be responsible for that, do you?"

"No sir."

"Then get a hurry on."

As he alighted from his car at the studio Thicknesse heard three huge explosions. One after the other. He again looked at his watch. It was 10.50 a.m. He knew that it would take his men about ten minutes to clear the debris and that the traffic would then start to flow normally. And that would be the end of the Great Traffic Jam. His timing couldn't have been more perfect. As he rode up in the lift his mind was far away. In the Caribbean where he knew that he would soon be buying the country club.

At precisely eleven o'clock Commander Thicknesse appeared on the screen and announced that traffic was once again flowing along the main arteries of London. Then, after roundly condemning the Deadheads for causing all the congestion with their vans, he thanked everyone for their patience and endurance over the last forty-eight hours. "Furthermore, it gives me great pleasure to announce that there has not been a single death due to a traffic accident since Friday night. This is the longest period since 1933 when there hasn't been a traffic death somewhere in London. So perhaps it was all worth it," he said with a smile. "At least it was for me," he thought to himself.

■
———

After he saw his mate's performance on television Slick Nick made his way to the diverse betting shops where he had obtained incredibly long odds that the traffic jam would end at 11 a.m. Monday. The men and women at the various windows paid him out with a range of looks that went from the surly to the downright envious. He put each fresh bundle of notes into his suitcase and then went home to count it.

"Holy Hottentots!" he thought. "I'd be ripe pickings for a robber." In such a state of mild panic he rang his friend and partner at the Traffic Office.

"Take a flight to the Caymans and put it in our joint bank account there," said the Commander. "Safer to take it on the 'plane with you than to put it through the British banking system where it could be traced. You should have enough in the suitcase to buy an air ticket. First Class" He roared with laughter at his own joke.

■
———

"My word, Commander Thicknesse and his men have done a great job clearing all that traffic," said Mrs. Thatcher's secretary. "I think he should be given a little something in the

Queen's Birthday Honours List."

"Yes, of course," replied the Prime Minister. "We all owe him a great deal. Put him down for a knighthood and I'll submit it with all the others."

"No, I don't think it should be anything as grand as a knighthood."

"Why not?"

"Well, the other knights might object. After all, cops are not exactly out of the top drawer, are they? Or even the second to top drawer. The others might regard it as a debasement of their particular order and we don't want to upset the knights extant, do we?"

"Oh, all right then. Give him an M.B.E. They're a more cosmopolitan bunch.

And don't forget a knighthood for the Secretary of State for Transport. It was his timely intervention in lighting the fire and ringing all the bells that warned the people to stay at home and not contribute further to the congestion."

"Even though he burned down most of Hampstead Heath?"

"Oh yes. The trees will grow again. And I thought that his television statement was quite superb. I do like a man with a good grasp of history. He put the blame where it fairly and squarely lies. King Charles the Second should have spent less time with his mistresses and more time studying Wren's road plan. If he had accepted it we wouldn't have had all this trouble over the week-end."

Meanwhile over at Transport another post-mortem on the traffic jam was taking place.

"What's our current funds position? Will we be over budget or are we likely to show a small surplus at the end of the financial year?" Humphrey Granville-Gore asked his financial secretary.

"Current projections suggest that we'll finish up with a surplus of a few thousand pounds — maybe up to fifty thousand — which we will be able to hand back to the Chancellor."

"Come now, think of all the funds that the Chancellor has at his disposal. Everybody's taxes. He'll regard the return of a mere fifty thousand as an insult. I've got a better idea."

"What's that, sir?"

"I think that we should build a monument to the Great Traffic Jam — just like they erected the Monument in the City to commemmorate the Great Fire."

"And where would you suggest that this monument should be built?"

"Well, obviously where the traffic jam began."

"Unfortunately, sir, there seems to be quite a bit of dispute on that score. The Tories claim that the trouble started on the Thames bridges, Mister Telford-Weston asserted in the Daily Troublemaker that it all began on the Wembley roundabout, while Commander Thicknesse insists that it was caused by all the Deadheads' vans outside Wembley Arena."

"Well, I'm prepared to believe Mister Telford-Weston. We went to the same school."

"So you think that we should build a monument alongside the Wembley roundabout?"

"Not alongside it. Right on it. At the very spot where the Mercedes broke down and started the whole thing. On the road itself."

"But that would cause even more congestion!"

"Nonsense. There are at least two other lanes. And, besides, there aren't enough statues in that part of London; they're all in the City and the West End. It would be culturally uplifting for the people to drive past a well-built statue on their way to work."

"And what would you put up? A model of an internal combustion engine?"

"No, I was thinking of something a bit more personal. More homely."

"What?"

"A life size image of myself swinging a golf club. After all, if I hadn't issued the instructions when I did, the jam would have been far worse and we might never have unjammed it. Think how terrible that would have been!"

"What a good idea, sir!" said his momentarily stunned private secretary. "Perhaps you should consider putting yourself atop a high column like Nelson. Then you could watch all the F.A. Cup finals at Wembley."

"I don't like football. I'm a rugby man. Oxford Blue in fact. And I don't think that I would be able to see as far as Twickenham from the Wembley roundabout. No, I think a base about five feet high would be appropriate. Just high enough for the people to be able to lay wreaths at my feet each year on the anniversary of my death.

A friend of mine has a daughter-in-law who is a sculptress. I've seen some of her work. It's very good. If I give her a commission now, then it should be ready by the summer. And the Queen could come and unveil it on a sunny day in July. Before she goes to Balmoral. I'm sure she could find time for that."

"Yes, I'm sure she could," said the private secretary.

"And now to the main issue of the day," said Humphrey Granville-Gore in a grave tone.

"And what is the main issue, sir?"

"Should I be in bronze or marble?"

■

Commander Thicknesse had his feet up on the armchair as he sucked on a bottle of lager while waiting for the Mid Evening News to come on the television. "I'll probably be on the screen again," he called to his short, dumpy wife who was in the kitchen making a bread and butter custard for to-morrow night's dessert.

It had been a long and satisfying day for the Commander. He had left his office at four o'clock to drive Nick to Heathrow for his flight to the Caymans on Dashington Airways Flight Number 972. Then he had called in at his football club for a few drinks and later drove himself home with an alcohol level that would have been slightly over the legal limit — if he had been pulled up and breathalysed — which he knew he never would be. He was now feeling more than a little merry as his wife came into the sitting room, took off her apron and sat down next to him to watch the News.

"I'm bound to be on first," he said as he took another swig from the brown bottle. But he wasn't.

When the chimes of Big Ben ended, the newsreader began by announcing that Dashington Airways Flight Number 972 had been blown up in mid-air over the Channel less than half an hour after leaving Heathrow. "Palestinian terrorists who boarded the 'plane at Athens and got off in London are believed to be responsible," he continued. "All passengers and crew are presumed to have been killed instantly and rescue services are currently searching the coast near Weymouth for debris. The only item that has been recovered intact is a large suitcase full of fifty pound notes which the police have stated 'was almost certainly drug money on its way out of Britain to be laundered'."

"What a terrible thing to happen!" exclaimed Mrs. Thicknesse in her strong Liverpudlian accent.

"Not good, not good," mumbled her husband as he got up to go out to the kitchen. "We'll just have to have another traffic jam. An even longer one with bigger odds."

A few miles away at the Inns of Court Myles and Fiona were attending a cocktail party in honour of the visiting American lawyers. It was an elegant and glittering occasion and the two great branches of the English speaking world were getting along famously. The Americans had a genuine interest in seeking out the English origins of their own common law while the British were impressed by the natural charm, vitality and informality of their trans-Atlantic cousins.

A young attorney from Arizona gasped audibly when Myles told him that they had been teaching law at Gray's Inn since the 1200s. "Hell, man, that's three centuries before Columbus sailed. And six centuries before the first settlers trekked into

Arizona. No wonder you Brits hold together so well - with institutions as strong as that."

"Yes," replied Myles, "and see that old gentleman sitting in the armchair over there — he's the current Treasurer of the Inn."

"Looks as if he's been around since the 1200s too," laughed the Arizonan. "I must say, he's got plenty of condition on him for a relic."

"Yes, well it has been whispered that he stood on the wharf at Plymouth and blew outwards to provide wind for the Mayflower when she sailed."

"Then in that case he did a sterling job. One of my mother's forebears was a passenger."

"Yes, and one of my mother's forebears was a passenger on a boat that came to England."

"What kind of boat?"

"A Viking longboat."

"Is that why you've got fair hair?"

"Guess so."

Although his gout prevented him from getting out of his armchair, the Treasurer of Gray's Inn was displaying his usual gracious charm to all the overseas guests. "And how are you enjoying your stay in our grand old country?" he asked Lurlene Puncher as she was ushered into his presence and introduced as "Florida's most successful prosecuting attorney".

"It's really great now that the traffic jam is over," she replied.

"Traffic jam? What traffic jam?"

"Oh, my God!" gasped Lurlene as she fell down in a swoon.